FERVOR

Omegaverse Romance

Omega Assassins Club

Book One

KIKI BURRELLI

CONTENTS

A note from Kiki:

While there is no less steam or heart in Fervor, there is more violence than is found in the average Kiki Burrelli book. Please use your discretion and be aware this book contains themes of graphic violence as well as mentions of abuse and rape.

CHAPTER ONE
Wynn

The bass from the music blasting out onto the patio vibrated throughout my body. Overhead, there wasn't a cloud in the night sky. Only the brightest stars shone this deep in the city. The penthouse level of the hotel had a rooftop infinity pool and outdoor entertaining area lit with tiki torches, exclusively available to the richest, most powerful alphas.

I bent over, sending the leering alpha sitting behind me a wink while I reached for the bottle of high-end vodka. I poured a generous amount into the shaker and added a splash of vermouth and a bit of olive juice before popping the cap on and spinning back to face my audience.

The alpha wasn't alone. His buddies, all of them just as confident and debauched, stared at me as I sauntered back to where my alpha sat. I'd chosen my silver sequined booty shorts for several reasons: because it sparkled and because the shorts clung to my ass in that magical way that somehow made the twin globes seem perkier.

The alpha held out his empty martini glass in the space between our bodies. He smirked when I gave the shaker a little jiggle. The ice from inside had condensed along the stainless-steel outside, making my fingertips freeze a little to the surface. "Need a refill?" I asked, smiling shyly.

The alpha liked that. His friends did too if their groaning was any indication. I breathed in the testosterone, and my wolf snarled. To him, that smelled like danger. To me, it was a sign of what was to come. "Normally, I'm the one to do the filling, but I'll let it slide this time," the alpha guffawed as his friends grunted their laughter.

They were salivating in the palm of my hand, and I basked in the power that sent coursing through me.

I opened my mouth and spread my lips around the shaker lid. I sucked, my cheeks hollowing as I removed the lid with my mouth. More groans came from the peanut gallery. One muttered something about how I'd be slobbering on that dick later, and while I had to give him points for eagerness, those points were canceled out by his crude manner.

"Don't worry, men, there's enough of me to go around," I told the five of them with a smile. Four if I didn't count the main alpha, but he was the reason I was here. He needed to be counted.

"Don't they all say that at first?" the alpha sitting closest to my mark whispered in his ear.

My hand jerked, spilling some of the cocktail onto my alpha's hand instead. He snarled, batting the shaker from my grip. It skittered along the patio, the contents exploding onto the stucco and into the infinity pool that looked over the glistening city.

"I'm sorry!" I cried out, dropping to my knees as the alpha grabbed a handful of my hair.

He jerked on it once, as if to show me how much control he had over my body. A motion like that said, *I could hurt you if I wanted to.* I whimpered and parted my lips, peering up at him.

The hard lines on the alpha's face softened. He smiled. With his other hand, he caressed his knuckles down my cheek. "This is a beautiful face," he murmured. "Pouty, come-fuck-me lips. Smooth skin begging for my mark.

And, *damn*, those eyes. I want to see that golden gaze looking up at me as you choke on my cock." The last part was said more roughly and punctuated by sharp jerks on my hair.

I cried out but didn't dare try to pull away.

"C'mon, Dirk, stop hogging the entertainment," one of the other alphas called out. There was another round of laughter, sounds of zippers being pulled and clothing falling to the ground. My pulse raced, making my heart pound. This was always the worst part.

Dirk released me with a jerk. "On your knees, omega. Assume your rightful position before your alpha."

Cheers and jeers came from the peanut gallery. I looked at the poky stucco. I was only wearing my shorts, and the sharp edges would dig into my knees in seconds. "Could I get a towel?" I asked softly.

Dirk and the rest laughed at my audacity. "A towel? Fucking, mouthy omega." He loomed over me, using his larger frame as the weapon it was. "I'll tell you what. You suck my dick and *earn* your towel."

A cool wind blew by. During the day, when it was sweltering and sticky, I would've appreciated that wind. Now, with so much exposed skin, it made goosebumps pop up my arms. "I don't think I want to do this," I said, wrapping my slim arms around my body.

"Does someone give these bitches a script? The same thing every time. They're into it until the fun starts, and then it's all I have a headache, I need a towel." The alpha speaking stepped forward as his friends all did the same. Soon, they were circled around me, all of them at least a foot taller than myself and much more muscular.

I raised my hands in front of me as my wolf went quiet, focused. "Wait, I said I wasn't sure."

"You don't seem real bright, so I'm going to spell it out for you," Dirk growled. He downed the rest of his martini and threw the glass down behind him, shattering the crystal into thousands of glittering pieces. "I've paid for

3

you—"

"I'm not a whore," I spat back, but my voice sounded high and reedy.

"Aren't you? In that fucking getup? I've been paying for your drinks all night, got you this room, and now that me and my pals want to enjoy ourselves a little, you're suddenly so chaste? Omegas like you think they can tease and poke the bear. You know what happens when you poke a bear?" He dropped his pants and grabbed his hard dick. It was thick, veiny and engorged. "You get the horns."

The alphas crowded in all at once. I cowered down in a squatting position, reaching for the third reason I liked these shorts. The shiny hid the sharp.

I slipped my finger into the grip of the folding knife, pulling it free and flicking out the blade in one fluid motion. The world around me quieted, blocking any sensation that wasn't in my immediate vicinity. My wolf snarled in that discordant yet gleeful way. This wasn't what we'd been born to do, not what we were made for, but it was what we'd become. I whipped my arm around so quickly Dirk didn't even cry out until the turgid member he'd been holding slipped free of his grip like a greased pig running to freedom only to flop to the ground with an obscene splat.

He looked down at his hand, confused by its sudden emptiness and the warm red that poured out of him. Only then did he scream. It was high pitched and not at all like the manly grunting he'd been doing most of the night.

The other alphas, all in various stages of undress, caught on to the fact that the night was no longer going how they'd expected. Their shocked gasps quickly turned into growling, but I was ready for this part. I swung my left leg out, tripping the alpha on one side while swiping around with my right hand to nick the femoral artery of the alpha on the other side. I surged up and slammed my shoulder into his chest, sending him tripping back and into the pool.

The two that had been behind me rushed back to their pants, retrieving their guns. One fired a shot, that ricocheted off the stucco, sending up a small poof of dust and debris. I reached for my second knife. This one was thinner, more streamlined. I sent that knife through the air without watching it hit its mark. I knew what I'd aimed for. Sure enough, his body dropped in my peripheral.

"You fucking bitch!" the other alpha who'd been behind me cried out. He dropped, shifting into his animal form.

And they tried to say all omegas were the same? When cornered and threatened, alphas always shifted, somehow expecting their animal form to achieve what they could not as a human.

For a reason I'd never know, our shifter counterparts were like mirrors into the man inside. My own wolf was all black—save for a patch of white at my chest—with golden eyes. He hunted efficiently but not cruelly and preferred hunting other predators.

This alpha's wolf was squat and mangy. He had bald patches behind his ears and along his back. When he snarled at me, drool dripped from his jaw as a rancid odor filled the air. This was a wolf that thrived on other things being weaker than he was. Thanks to the genetic lottery, he'd been born an alpha, strong, dominant, and to him that meant he could prey on the weak when really, he should've protected them.

Today, he'd pay for that mistake.

He lunged, jaws open, preparing to use his sharp teeth to rip out my throat. I ducked to the side, my height an advantage since it made it easier for me to reach under him as he nearly sailed over my head. I thrust up, lodging my knife into his sternum while holding on with both hands and letting gravity do the rest.

His body fell, but I wasn't finished.

Two were left: Dirk, and the alpha I'd tripped at the

start of it all. He'd gotten time to see me work, witnessing one of his buddies moaning on the ground dickless and another currently filling the pool with red.

His eyes widened as I took a small step toward him. I'd taken some blood splatter from stabbing the wolf over my head, and it speckled my bare chest and sequined shorts. The alpha turned and ran toward the wall of glass of the hotel room, his nervous yelps a far cry from the guffawing, slobbering man he'd been just ten minutes ago.

I prioritized, deciding to finish my original target, Dirk, first before chasing the last alpha down. When I turned to Dirk, his face was pale as a summer cloud and twisted into an expression of pure loathing.

"You'll pay for this, you bitch," he snarled thickly, lifting his gun.

He fired, and I dodged to the side. The fleeing alpha behind me cried out just as he'd reached the elevator. His body dropped revealing a small splash of blood in the middle of the elevator doors that split in two as they opened. The alpha's body slumped down between the doors.

"Thanks," I said, swinging my left leg in a low roundhouse that kicked the gun from Dirk's weakening grip. Technically, the job was finished, Dirk would bleed out, and I would get paid. But *I* wasn't finished.

I took my time, sauntering around Dirk, standing over his body in much the same way he'd done to me. "This didn't turn out how you wanted," I said softly.

"F-Fuck you!" Dirk spit the curse out.

"If you had your way, I'd still be on my knees and you'd be using me however you wanted. All of you would, and my screams of no wouldn't matter, would they? They didn't for all the others."

Ten omegas in total. Ten innocent humans who had been lured into Dirk's web. Used, abused, and discarded. Only two of those omegas had survived their night with Dirk and his pals.

This gasping, growling man at my feet had been just like most every other alpha, thinking his superior strength and size made *him* superior.

Maybe before that was true. But not anymore. Push a group of people down enough and soon, there's nowhere to go but up.

"This is revenge? A vendetta?" Dirk whined.

"No," I said softly, shaking my head and smiling. "This is justice."

I finished him swiftly. My aim wasn't to cause pain, though pain was generally unavoidable in my line of work. I waited for his last breath before closing his eyes and then tapping the comm link at my ear that would open the signal to Remington, a beta as well as my field handler.

"Report," Remington's deep voice sounded in my ear.

"Targets eliminated, five in total. No unwanted casualties."

"Five?" Remington echoed. "I thought the plan was to get them one on one."

I looked around at the mayhem and mess. "They wanted a party," I said with a shrug.

"Mhmm, and you were more than willing to go along with it. Do you require medical assistance?" he asked tiredly, like he was expecting the answer.

"Negative."

"I'll send in the crew," Remington said, but with a hesitation that made me think there was more.

"What is it?" I asked, using a bottle of water to rinse most of the blood from my body. I found my shirt and slipped it over my head.

"You've been assigned your next target. This isn't a land and stab, though. You'll need to collect intel. I'll send what I got from Taft. They need specific information from the mark before you dispatch him. Which means you'll need to gain access into his home and workspaces until you find it. Some sort of tracking code, unheard of before now."

I frowned, having only located one of my plain gray loafer slip-ons. I searched the area, finding my other shoe under the table inches away from a pool of blood. I'd lost more shoes that way.

Land and stabs were my specialty: in and out, lots of mess, lots of fuss. Since graduating training—where we were all tested and evaluated on a series of information gathering tests—the more intel-heavy missions always went to one of my omega brothers. All River needed to do was blink his baby blues at an alpha, and they tripped over themselves to give him what he wanted. And Van could turn on the charm brighter than anyone else in the world.

I was less charming and more stabby. It was how I liked it.

"I know what you're thinking, and yes, Taft confirmed twice that he wants you on this."

"Does the target meet the criteria?" I asked, having found both shoes and my shirt among the chaos. I wasn't in a hurry since Dirk had made sure with the hotel staff his *activities* wouldn't be interrupted. No one would dare come up here with what he paid them. I could've screamed my head off for hours, and every person in this hotel would've looked the other way.

I growled, but the employees and guests were safe from me. The Omega Assassins Club didn't kill without discretion. I wouldn't be an agent if they did. But, all around the world, omegas faced decades of oppression. Daily, more legislation was passed that took more omega rights away. The OAC had been founded from necessity. Fight or die. And we were done dying.

Every target I'd ever taken out had a list of crimes against omegas as long as twenty of Dirk's severed dicks. Though not every omega employed at the OAC cared about what an alpha had done to land in their sights, for me, it was a necessity. I needed to be angry. That was the only way I could handle the endless guilt that always followed.

"Not much here. Name is Magnus, alpha, CEO of a tech security firm and is on the brink of releasing new technology that will make every omega in the world trackable by any alpha with the right app. Before you dispatch the target, the client wants the program code so they can destroy it."

I snarled. This dick wanted to make it so omegas couldn't hide? There was no end to how bad that would be. Omegas hiding from their abusers, omegas in heat in search of a safe, secluded space. None of them—none of *us* would be safe.

"Send me the file. I'll station at the safe house in this region and begin tomorrow."

Remington grunted, and then the line went dead.

"Thanks for the party, boys," I whispered before disappearing down the service stairs. If I hurried, I might be able to get to the safe house and in the shower before cold guilt settled on my shoulders. I took a deep breath, hating that it was shaky on the exhale.

I was only playing the hand I was dealt. There wasn't anything else I could do to protect my fellow omegas except this. But in recent days, I'd had to remind myself of that, more and more.

CHAPTER TWO
Magnus

"So I told him, you want forty-five percent, that deal better include free use of your mate," Jorge said, immediately laughing at his own story.

While his head was thrown back, the slim omega at his side gave me a lusty look. He'd been shooting me bedroom eyes since he and Jorge had arrived for dinner.

I chuckled lightly while doing my best to ignore the omega's silent advances. I hadn't seen this particular companion with Jorge, but knew he had a pool of eager omegas waiting for a call and a few large bills. Jorge didn't so much love them and leave them as he used them and set them on the shelf for later. It wasn't a huge distinction, but it made the difference between whether we could be business partners or not.

If I'd known that starting my own security firm out of my parent's basement was going to wind up with me having to interact with the worst of the worst on a daily basis, I might've—

Who was I kidding? I would've done the exact same thing again. The end result of my efforts was what was important, and the journey to that point would just have to be endured.

But the other stuff? The fancy dinners and confining suits, the waifish omegas that hung off their alpha's arms like jewelry, that I could definitely do without. Which was why dinners like this were few and far between. I felt a tickle at my ankle and moved my other foot to scratch it when I realized the tickle at been Jorge's date, rubbing my leg with his bare foot. He wasn't an unattractive man. The omega wouldn't be with Jorge if he was. He had curly blond hair that looked like it would be soft to the touch and bright blue eyes that sparkled in the candlelight. His features were feline in nature, with his angular cheeks and lips that curved up in the corners.

He might as well be wearing a burlap sack over his head for how much of an effect he had on me. It was too difficult for me to look at him and not see his looks as what they really were: his armor. That, and he was Jorge's—for the night at least. Some alphas liked playing homewrecker, stealing omega mates away just because they could while exerting their dominance over other alphas, but that wasn't like me.

I moved my leg smoothly: not jerking it away, but not allowing myself to be fondled against my will.

"Hello, paging Magnus, your attention is needed in this conversation," Jorge said, smiling, but there was an annoyed edge. As an alpha, he was likely used to being paid attention to. As a long-term acquaintance and former co-owner, he was used to my lackluster behavior.

"My apologies," I replied, straightening my tie and taking a sip of water from the Swarovski crystal goblet. I would've been just as happy with a red plastic cup, but I'd learned early in my business that impressions of wealth and power were more important than actually having any of either.

Jorge laughed, but most of his annoyance was gone. That was another reason I liked him. He didn't hold a grudge. "You wish you were back home, huh? At the ole dive, drinking pints with the game on?" Hearing him talk about the life I'd come from, it was like he tried to make all I'd left behind sound not amazing.

"Yes, actually. But my work is in the city, so I am too."

"Unless you sell to Visadore. Then you can take your millions and buy not only the dive, but the entire neighborhood along with it."

I silenced my growl so it came out more of a low rumble. "Jorge, I will never sell. It's not just a business for me. I thought you knew that."

Jorge leaned back, turning his head to the omega at his side. The omega smiled at him sweetly, like he hadn't just been barking at my feet. Jorge cupped him around the nape, pulling closer to kiss him on the cheek. "You wouldn't know it, but this man right here, one of the most infuriating alphas you'll ever meet," Jorge said to the omega, mostly teasing, but there was always some truth.

"Really?" the omega purred. "I can't believe you. He seems so determined, strong…"

"Whoa now," Jorge replied with an easy laugh. "I should know better than to book dates from my prime pool when I'm going out with you, Magnus." To his escort he said, "I lose more omegas that way."

"Pardon me," I replied.

"Oh come now, Magnus, you can't take a little teasing?"

"I can take teasing, but unless you don't mind if I drop trou and handle my business right here, I should step away for a moment." I left the table and Jorge's laughter.

I picked my way through the restaurant, ignoring the glances I received from the other patrons. At places like this, no one ever wanted to be with who they were. They were all looking for the next step, the richer alpha, the more influential alpha. It was a brutal rat race with a prize at the end that I never understood. Prestige was just an eight-letter word, but so was pizzeria, and I knew which one I preferred.

My company was successful, but because we made useful product. Our password encryption services were far beyond what any other tech firm was offering. In the early days of the company, I had contacted notorious hackers and information brokers, paying them to attempt to break through my programs. The early years were a lot of trial, a lot of failure, but once success started, it didn't ever stop. Only recently had MattyCorp gotten the capital needed to truly begin testing the latest invention. And we were close, so close to changing the world.

"Excuse me," I said, bumping into a tall, thin man as we both attempted to walk into the bathroom. His scent was light and elusive, which only made me want to go in for a deeper, longer sniff.

"No problem," the man replied, his voice delicate like a spoon tapping against a glass to announce a toast.

I turned my head to get a better look, but he'd backed up, away from the door, standing against the wall with his head down and his hands clasped in front of him. I knew about a thousand alphas, many of them sitting behind me, that would've been thrilled to have an omega present so obediently. But not me.

"Omegas first," I said, standing to the side and sweeping my arm to the door in a welcoming gesture.

The omega didn't react. In fact, it didn't even look like he was breathing for at least five seconds. Then it was like what I'd said clicked, and his face jerked up, giving me my first look. My first thought was that I'd seen this face before. He was young, likely just old enough to order alcohol legally. His lips were full and a shade of red that reminded me of raspberries ripened in the sun. His skin shimmered almost as brightly as his golden eyes. While I couldn't forget a face like that, I also couldn't place him. "Omegas first?" he asked, like the words in that order made no sense.

I smiled and nodded as he furrowed his brow and pouted. I understood that my actions were a little outside of what he was likely used to, but he looked at me like I'd transformed into a different being entirely. He tilted his head in a way that made it seem like he was working out a fifty-sided Rubik's cube. "Thank you," he replied finally, barely more than a whisper.

I waited several seconds so he wouldn't feel rushed by my presence behind him and then entered, going to the urinal. He wasn't standing there, meaning he must have gone into a stall and that I should start minding my own business while in the bathroom.

I unzipped before feeling someone behind me. For a fraction of a second, I thought it was the same golden-eyed man, but the scent that hit my nose wasn't delicate or elusive. It was overpowering.

"I picked up on the code," Jorge's omega murmured in my ear.

I tucked myself in and zipped up before turning to him. He was much shorter than I was, meaning I had to look down as he peered up. "Did Jorge send you?" I asked, not because I thought Jorge would, but because I wanted to make the point that he was here with my business partner, not with me.

"No, I told him I needed to wash up." The omega smiled sweetly. "Obviously his purpose was to bring me to you."

"Mhm," I said, stepping to the side to the sinks. I hadn't gone, but there was no way I was going to pull myself out in front of this omega. He'd take it as an invitation. "Look, I'm sorry if I gave you the wrong impression—"

"You didn't. You gave me the right one," the omega replied, rubbing against me and further reminding me of a cat.

"—But I am not interested." I kept my tone low and even. I wasn't trying to embarrass the poor omega, but I needed to make it clear that whatever he thought was happening between us wasn't.

"You mean I don't tempt you?" he said, blinking his big blue eyes. A move like that might've worked on a lesser

14

alpha. "My heat's coming, I'll need someone to keep me warm, fill my aching holes. You don't want that?" As he spoke, I smelled his pheromones—light, a glimpse into how he would be during a full heat. My dick hardened, but it was purely a biological response, the alpha wolf in me recognizing the needy omega wolf in him. This omega didn't see it that way, though. He surged forward, pressing our bodies flush together as I backed into the sink.

Anger built in me which only made me harder because, yeah, I wasn't a dick alpha, but I was still an alpha with a dick. Passionate emotions—anger, desire, all of it— seemed to signal the same response in my body, to conquer by fucking all else into submission. I took a deep breath. I didn't want to hurt this omega, mentally or physically, but he was proving more difficult to handle than most.

"Omegas talk, you know," he continued. "And baby, they *whisper* about you."

I'd been downtown for just over fifteen years, moving downtown after my little basement business got its first big client. Those first few years had been about scrounging, trying to afford to be where the action was. In all that time, I'd dated, had been set up by friends, and now I was beginning to suspect most of the *friends* Jorge had set me up with had just been omegas from his personal pool.

"Well they can stop whispering," a light, tinkling voice replied. "He's taken, for now." The golden-eyed omega I'd ran into stepped out of the stall, sliding smoothly between me and Jorge's omega, effectively breaking us apart on his way to the sink. He washed his hands silently with sure, unhurried motions.

"Who are you?" Jorge's omega snapped. His voice wasn't quite as high or melodic now. It had a nasally edge that I imagined was closer to his natural tone. The whispery stuff was just an act. Like the rest of him.

"Wynn, like what I do," the omega replied.

I smirked and covered my mouth to hide my laugh.

"Wynn? Are you new to Wolf's Peak?"

"Yes and no. It's my first time in the establishment, though I must admit, I don't much like it."

Jorge's omega scowled. "Not rich enough for you?"

Wynn looked from me and then back to Jorge's omega. "The staff is too pushy."

Neither myself nor Jorge's omega could miss what the new omega, Wynn, was implying. Jorge had paid his omega to be here, both in cash and goods, I would bet the watch he wore now had been a gift from Jorge that very evening. "Are you implying—" Jorge's omega began.

But Wynn stepped smoothly forward, making me think he was a dancer or something similar. He stopped when his face was barely an inch from the other omega.

My wolf howled. That pervy beast expected a scene. I had to remind him we didn't live in porno land, and these two omegas weren't likely about to rip each other's clothes off. I got the idea that Jorge's omega couldn't handle Wynn even if they did. Wynn spoke with quiet authority. "You want to go back to your date. He pays you, which is better than what a lot of omegas get. Don't shit on that."

It wasn't that omegas didn't cuss, but more that they were never their authentic selves when alphas were around. Either from necessity or safety, they always acted gentler and quieter when alphas and even sometimes betas were present. But Wynn didn't seem to mind that I was there.

I fully expected Jorge's omega to argue. Instead, he dropped his gaze, as if he would if Wynn were an alpha demanding his respect. He nodded and mumbled something so quiet I couldn't hear, but Wynn heard and nodded. "You're a lucky one," Wynn said just loud enough for me to hear.

The other omega shuffled out, his face down as if he'd been thoroughly chastised. As Wynn turned around, the light from the closing bathroom door outlined his profile, bringing me back to years earlier, when my company had just begun to take off.

I had been in a bar, much lower scale than the establishment we were in now, but still several steps above a dive. At the time, Jorge was just my first big investor and not my business partner, and he'd insisted on sealing our deal with a night out. The scotch had flowed like water, and there'd been no shortage of pretty, young omegas longing to be invited to our table. I'd spotted one, noticing him mostly because of his age. Young. Too young to be where he was and definitely too young to be hanging off the old, gruff alpha he'd been with.

I hadn't had as much experience with the alpha businessman lifestyle, and my threshold for butting in had been leagues lower. I'd been *convinced* the too-young omega had been coerced into being there with the much older man and asserted as much when I spoke up—fueled by limitless scotch.

I'd gotten a bloody nose for my troubles and quite a few dings to my pride when it turned out the young omega *wanted* to be exactly where he was. He'd been a hooker, like Jorge's omega but with less pretense.

I growled, realizing that hooker and Wynn were the same person. They had to be. His eyes were a little darker, and his body had filled out. He was long and lean now, but I was sure he was the same omega as before.

And he wanted to lecture Jorge's omega on being bought?

My disappointment was so thick I could taste it, like drinking a glass of ice water on a hot day only to find it was saltwater.

Wynn however, smiled, oblivious to the fact that I was onto him. "I hope you don't mind. It sounded like you weren't into it. Though I wonder why you didn't put him in his place."

I growled, both angry at what I'd discovered and at the phrase Wynn had used. *His place.* Those words were like an echo, luring me back to the past. "We're not all assholes," I replied, turning back to the urinal. While I'd been hesitant to continue with the other omega around, with Wynn, it felt like a challenge. I unzipped myself and pulled my dick out while Wynn waited.

Finishing, I put myself back together and then went to the sink, washing my hands silently. I'd met hundreds of hookers on outings like this one. Escorts, prostitutes, whatever they were called, they were the same, and while I didn't fault the omegas for doing what they needed to do to be safe and survive, why did this one have to?

I felt his eyes on me, watching my movements like we'd switched positions and he was the hunter.

"I'm heading home now," I told him.

Wynn smirked. Before it had seemed so real, but now, it felt flat. "Shall I join you?" he asked brazenly. But not so brazen that his voice didn't dip with uncertainty at the end.

I wished I could believe even that hint of nerves. But he looked to be no more than twenty-one, and I had seen him at least a decade ago, give or take a few months in either direction. That would have put Wynn not only at a grotesque age to be a sex worker, but now, so many years later, he was likely more experienced at fooling alphas than even Jorge's omega. "No, you shall not," I replied, watching Wynn wince before he could hide it.

"I am sorry if I poked my muzzle where it didn't belong."

"You didn't. Thank you for helping me with that omega."

Wynn's eyes widened in shock. Because I thanked him? That just made my anger burn more brightly.

I hated that even though I knew who this omega was, *what* this omega was, I still wanted him. Not just in a latent alpha-wants-an-omega sort of way, but this omega in particular. He'd intrigued me from the very first moment, except now I knew that first moment had been years ago and not minutes.

I forced my body to the door, stopping before pushing

through. "You have a way to get home safely?" I asked without turning around. I didn't think I'd be able to. I'd take one more look at those golden eyes or get one more whiff of his luscious scent and forget that I cared that this omega would never belong to me alone—only to the man with the biggest wallet.

"I do," he replied, and while I still wasn't looking, I could imagine the almost regal way he would hold his body as he replied.

I nodded curtly, finally pushing the door open. I'd make some excuse to Jorge. He was used to me bailing early on social functions. Keeping my promise to myself, I didn't look back. But as the door shut and Wynn was blocked from my view, I wondered why I felt like I'd made a   huge   mistake.

CHAPTER THREE
Wynn

"He made sure you had a safe way home and then...left?" River asked, his blond curls bouncing as he climbed the stair stepper. It was a brutal machine, and most days I would take torture over an hour of endless climbing. But River—the youngest of our group—had been training at the Omega Assassins Club since he was a young boy. Now that he was a graduated assassin, he was as fit as the rest of us. Even if he looked like an angel fresh from heaven. A part of our job required us to be stereotypically appealing, which meant slim bodies and firm asses.

"Well, you must've wiggled under his skin if he cared about that," Van said between lightning-fast punches. He skipped around the defense dummy, landing blow after blow to its head, neck, and abdomen. His dark red hair was wet along his brow and nape from sweat as his green eyes narrowed at the dummy in concentration.

I grumbled at the corkboard target on the other side of the room. "I wasn't trying to wiggle under his skin, Van. I was trying to get to his apartment."

Zed, the fourth graduate assassin in our team, was doing sit-ups in the corner. "Why'd Taft give you that mission anyway? You're shit at subtlety."

I snarled, lobbing a training knife in his direction. Technically, it could have hurt him since the blade was pointed to stick into the corkboard, but I trusted my skills and his. Sure enough, the knife twirled so it was handle-first when Zed batted it out of the air mid-sit-up. "I asked Remington the same question. He just said that Taft demanded it."

"Maybe he thought it was a cake mission and he wanted to reward you," River suggested while upping the intensity. He looked like an angel, but was clearly a masochist.

"Or he thought it was a cake mission and was glad it was finally one you could handle." Nolan, the last—and most unpleasant—member of our team walked in. He was a little older than the rest of us at twenty-four, having sought the OAC out by name at a later age than when the rest of us had been recruited. We'd been invited into the OAC. He had begged to train as an agent.

The rest of us had been scouted and chosen for various reasons. I'd been in the social system. Both of my parents were dead from overdoses. While my seven years as their omega son hadn't been great, the years that followed had quickly turned cruel. Things came to a head when I finally fought back against the alpha who had been paid by our government to take care of me but had spent that money on beer and weed while using me how he liked. At nine I bit his tongue off when he shoved it in my mouth for the last time.

I'd been sent to juvie, fighting for my life as much there as I had on the outside. It had taken about a week for Remington to find me and offer me this life. I'd never looked back.

Every omega here had a story like mine, and it was our combined mission to stop what had happened to us from happening to as many other omegas as possible.

Like Dirk, I thought, trying not to wince from the

memory. *He would've already forgotten what he'd done to you and would have moved on to the next. You saved lives.* I knew that was true, but it was getting harder to believe it was enough.

If only we could all be betas, in a fluid state, able to be exactly what they wanted at any time: alpha, omega, neither, both. The world was open to them—except for the fact that to reproduce they had to choose a state and stay that way. But who cared about having kids when the tradeoff was living free? Alphas treated most betas with vaguely concealed disdain, but that was still better than the way they craved ownership over omegas.

"You're late, Nolan," Van told him, swinging his leg around for a kick to the dummy's head that knocked the entire thing over.

"Mission from Taft," Nolan replied importantly. "He'll confirm if you don't believe me."

Van shot me an exasperated look before replying. "Why shouldn't I believe you? You're still late, and we're on rotation. Wait behind River, and you can take the stepper in Wynn's place when we switch."

I shot Van a grateful look. He knew my hatred for the vile machine. I wasn't able to exercise on it as much as the others anyway. My body would bulk up too much, making me less effective at slipping into the places I needed to be—normally under a horrible alpha's arm. Even as we trained to keep our smaller bodies strong enough to fight back, we had to worry, constantly calculating how much space we could take up in this world before it became too much.

"Whatever. Taft wants you in his office anyway, Wynn," Nolan replied, stretching his arm over his head. His curly brown hair was pulled back into a low, short ponytail.

"Was that the mission Taft sent you on, to tell Wynn to go to his office?" River asked quietly.

"What if it was, fucking punk?" Nolan snapped.

Van, Zed, and myself all snarled, spinning and

crouching. Zed's fangs grew into elongated points over his lip in mid-shift.

"Apologize," Van demanded.

Nolan lifted his chin in silent defiance. In the next moment, Zed shifted, bursting forward and slamming into Nolan's body with a loud thump. Snarls followed as Nolan shifted, snapping and scratching at Zed in return. Tufts of hair flew up in the air like clumps of soft snow. Zed's wolf was espresso brown with a white stomach. He was stockier as a wolf than in his other form, while Nolan's wolf, a mix of browns and blacks, always looked greasy.

"What is going on here?" Taft's voice bellowed throughout the training room.

Nolan and Zed quieted, shifting back into their human counterparts and reaching for their sweats. I tried not to look at the large scar that spread across the width of Zed's stomach, red and puckered like a violent smile. For as many years as we'd been training together, he had never once told any of us on his team the story of how he'd come across such an injury, but it didn't take a genius to figure out it was related to why he was here.

"I was just doing what you asked when they attacked me," Nolan whined, sounding like he should be the youngest of their group instead.

Taft's eyes went from River, to Van, and then me. "Wynn, what happened?" he asked with his deep voice. It was as if the sound of his words carried their own weight, dropping to the ground and remaining there like statues. Part of that was his alpha status, and part of that was just Taft's natural magnetism. And while it might have seemed odd that an organization full of omegas fighting back against alpha oppression was led by an alpha, the truth of our world was that an organization like ours needed eager investors, men who believed in our mission. Not only were omegas forbidden from keeping large sums of money, but most alphas, even those alphas dedicated to our cause, simply wouldn't do business with an omega. The OAC founders were tasked with equipping us with effective leaders, allowing us to bridge that gap and get the money we needed to operate.

"Nolan was rude to River. We were correcting that," I replied, my unblinking gaze on Nolan the whole time.

"Why were you correcting that behavior and not River?" Taft asked without anger or malice.

"Sir, I would have," River replied. "But everyone responded so quickly."

It was true. The three of us, myself, Van, and Zed, doted on River. He was the kid of our group, and while we didn't doubt his abilities as an effective assassin—with that face and body he could get into rooms the rest of us could only dream of—we protected him above all others.

"Do you all hear River? He felt more than capable to defend himself, and by defending him, you have all robbed him of that chance. If anyone owes him an apology, it is the three of you. And before you smile any wider, Agent Nolan, I sent you here with the direction to send Wynn to me, and yet…"

"I told him!" Nolan replied. "He refused."

Taft nodded, scratching his strong jaw before tapping the divot at the end of his chin. "I'll remember you have no authority in your team the next time I need something done." He turned, silencing any response Nolan might've come up with.

I saluted the rest of my team and trotted behind Taft, following him to his office on the other side of the training compound. Continuing training and mission debriefings all happened in this building, creatively named Building A, while our barracks and communal living spaces were in the building on the other side of the courtyard, Building B. Graduated teams were allowed off-base housing, but we only stayed in our own apartments when we were on leave, which wasn't often. Our team was our pack family—where else would we go during the holidays?

"Sit down, Wynn," Taft commanded.

I took the seat on the other side of his large desk. A chrome monitor sat on a swivel, and he pushed it my direction, showing me the image on the screen.

"Magnus Gray, CEO and founder of MattyCorp," Taft began.

I'd noticed the unusual business name in the file Remington had sent over. "Do you have any information on why he named the company that?" I asked.

Taft sat on the edge of the desk, his knees at my face level. He peered down the straight bridge of his nose, boring into me with his black eyes. I often wondered what Taft's wolf counterpart would look like. It would have black hair, like he did. But would it be as glossy as the hair on his head? Wolves mirrored the personality beneath. Would he be patchy and mangy like that alpha from my last mission? Or would he be as statuesque as a beast as he was as a man? "Does it matter what he calls his company, Wynn? Is that the information you're looking for?"

I sat straighter, folding my hands in my lap. "No, sir, that doesn't matter. I was just...curious, I guess."

"You were curious," Taft repeated. He bent at the middle, resting his elbows on his thighs and bringing his face closer. I concentrated on the angular line of his jaw, roughened with a day's worth of growth. "You were curious about a man who is actively developing technology to further enslave you and your kind?"

I dropped my face, my cheeks reddening with shame. Not because of my question, but because of the blossoming intent behind my question that Taft had immediately picked up on. I was curious about Magnus. Bumping into him at the bathroom entrance as I'd done had been no accident. I'd expected anger, had been ready for it. But he'd responded with something else, something that had made my body feel light.

"Did I make a mistake putting you on this mission, Wynn?" Taft asked, his voice coming from much closer. His heavy hand landed on my shoulder and caressed down

25

to my elbow, giving it a little shake. "Look at me, agent."

I schooled my face into a blank expression before looking up. Or, at least, I tried to. But some people were harder to fool than others. My team, for instance, and Taft. The founders had brought him into the OAC over five years ago and from the first day he'd found reasons to call me into his office.

But recently, those office visits contained more touching than they had in years passed. "I failed my first attempt," I said, hoping that if I couldn't hide the guilt I was beginning to feel more often, that I could at least redirect his assumptions. "He rejected me." But not right away. No, right away he'd been kind, polite, gentle. He'd waited outside of the bathroom for me to enter while most alphas would've barged in before or right after me, pressing up against my ass to exert their power.

"Then he is evil and an idiot," Taft murmured. His hand had released my elbow and trailed down to the thin, nearly translucent skin of my inner wrist.

I shivered. "That tickles," I said as my wolf perked his ears and began to pay attention. He didn't much like Taft, but I always thought that was because Taft was an alpha. Except my wolf had been more curious than untrusting with Magnus.

But Taft was a busy man, overseeing the missions of every active omega team as well as the progress of the new omegas in training. Every few months, a new team was assembled and began the years' long process of education. Depending on the age of the recruit, there was an initial training and orientation that could last several years. Based on the recruit's progress, they were slowly introduced to field training. I'd begun my field training at ten, less than a year from when my initial training began—and still held the youngest and shortest record. Those missions were information-based only.

The years that followed were about evaluation and continual mental and physical growth. When I was fifteen,

I got my first land and stab, a seventy-year-old alpha who liked to take young omegas into his home and do horrible things. I'd come out of that with a black eye, covered in blood—not mine—and a thirst for more. I'd gotten a taste of how alphas must feel—the power, the *vindication*.

Which brought me to now. Only in the last year had the guilt really started, popping its unwanted head up at the most inopportune times.

"How are you sure all of these alphas, all of these targets are as bad as the clients say they are?" I asked and the fingers that had been making small circles on my inner wrist stopped.

"Why do you ask?"

I shrugged, pulling my hand free and folding it with the other on my lap. "I don't know, I just…sometimes it gets harder to justify the things we do. But as long as it's for the greater good—"

Taft stood, walked to the wall to grab one of the chairs and pulled it closer. He sat in front of me, his knees nearly bumping against mine. "You've been in the OAC for around twelve years, haven't you? Longer than my own time here. I can't imagine everything you've seen, been subjected to. And that's ignoring the events that led to you being recruited in the first place. You bit an alpha's tongue off, correct?"

I nodded, keeping all emotion from my face.

"And in that time, have you seen horrors committed against omegas lessen?"

I shook my head. If anything, more laws had been passed granting omegas fewer rights. We weren't legally able to own property without an alpha's approval. We weren't able to have large sums of money in our own names. Every law passed under the guise of making omegas safer was really only further attempts to restrain us. Our bodies may have been weaker, but our minds weren't.

And my body wasn't either, not if I used it correctly.

"I can see how it can feel like the work we do is for nothing, but instead, you should look at it like tiny victories. You saved any future omegas from being subjected to brutal rape and torture by eliminating your last target. When you eliminate this one, you will be doing even more for omegas. Not just one or two, Wynn. You'll save the lives of thousands." Taft reached over, cupping my cheek with his rough palm.

While my life was rich with conflict and violence, it lacked in kind embraces and gentle touches. I pushed into his palm, my eyes fluttering closed for a brief moment until my wolf snarled and I jerked my head upright and out of Taft's grasp. "Thank you," I blurted, launching to my feet. "I needed that reminder."

Taft stood as well, angling his body between me and the door.

My wolf growled. He was more active since bumping into Magnus, and I wondered if he was that eager to eliminate the target, or if there was something else going on. But then, my wolf never fully trusted another until he'd witnessed them in their wolf form.

"I'm always here for you, Wynn. Don't think I haven't seen your drive, your dedication to the OAC. There are big things in your future, but I also know that this job is not just difficult physically, but mentally as well. Don't let small worries turn into big issues. Come to me, Wynn, for *anything*."

I wasn't imagining the emphasis he'd put on 'anything,' but I also didn't know what assumptions to make from such a statement. As an alpha, he was used to being listened to, sought out. Was this an extension of that? I pushed the thoughts from my mind. I didn't have time for Taft worries now. The rest of my day would be spent figuring out what had gone wrong with my first meeting with the target and then fixing whatever that was because there was no way I would let Magnus, the way he got under my skin, or my ever-present guilt stop me from saving omegas who couldn't save themselves.

CHAPTER FOUR
Magnus

"Did you send over the interface templates to the technicians?" I asked my secretary, Lloyd. He was a beta, an avid soccer player, and brewed his own beer in his basement—to his partner's annoyance.

Normally, Lloyd and I had an easy rapport, which was why he startled at my snappy tone. "I sent the files you gave me to the developers. That's where you told me to send them yesterday."

"The developers? No, we already got the final confirmation from them—"

While I spoke, Lloyd had started tapping on his monitor, spinning it so I could see the screen. "This is your message. You said developers. But I can get them to the technicians today…"

I looked over the screen, confirming what he'd said, and sighed. I'd been a mess for days, thinking about that young omega Wynn. He'd looked so confused at the end, likely wondering about my abrupt change in tone. That, or he simply wasn't used to being rejected. With his looks and charm, it was possible he never had been.

I didn't like thinking about that.

In fact, I hated thinking about that, and yet the images

were on a loop in my mind. Was he with an alpha now? Did he have regular customers as the ones Jorge frequented, or did he like to keep his clients fresh? If he'd been in the game for around a decade—since the last time I'd seen him—and never slept with the same alpha twice, he would've slept with the majority of the alphas in the city by now. I growled.

"I can do it right now, sir, just give me a moment," Lloyd replied, likely thinking I was growling at him.

Probably because I was still standing directly in front of him. It was just my head that was a million miles away. "No, thank you, I'll do it. This was my mistake, and I'll fix it."

Lloyd nodded but didn't turn back to his computer. He remained, looking up at me.

"Is there anything else?" I asked, hating that my distracted nature was making my employees hesitant around me. I never wanted them to be afraid in my presence. I mentally checked my posture, making sure my body language wasn't conveying anything I didn't mean to. Fighting my alpha nature was a constant struggle.

"Visadore sent another gift basket. I divvied up the gift basket items to the employees like you asked. But, sir, the card included some troubling language."

At least now Lloyd knew why I was growling. Visadore was a rival tech security firm. They'd been the big bad wolf when I'd first created my business and through the years had grown from the gold standard in tech security to a thorn in my side. My latest project, a result of over a decade of research—the whole reason I got into my business in the first place—was already getting the rumor mills going. A chip that an omega could implant on their person, discreetly and quickly, activating it during times of duress. The chip would begin recording audio as well as pinging closed-circuit cameras in the vicinity to begin recording their location. The final step was for the chip to send an automatic message to law enforcement in the area, signaling they required assistance.

It wouldn't do anything to fight the social climate when it came to omega rights, but it would make an omega's walk home or to school or *anywhere* that much safer. But Visadore wanted to use the tech as a tracking mechanism, to alter my invention into a weapon against omegas, not a tool. And I didn't care about how many threatening cards or messages they sent. The code and schematics for the highly complex technology were safe in my possession and would stay there. Even if Visadore got their hands on a case of chip prototypes, the tech was so layered and complex—both intentionally and by necessity—it would take their technicians years to figure it out. And by then I would own every patent for every step, every line of code necessary to create a functioning device.

But that did nothing to stop them from trying to strong-arm me now. First with ludicrous amounts of money and, when that didn't work, with intimidation. But unlike them, I didn't grow up with a silver bone in my mouth. I grew up in South Side, a small borough on the southernmost point of Wolf's Peak. The borough was so far from where I was geographically now that it felt like a different world altogether. My family and friends still lived there and likely always would. During the day, the streets were friendly, but at night, they had a law of their own. A law that some learned the hard way.

"Throw the card away and try not to let it worry you, Lloyd. It's all posturing. We are doing good work here, and that scares people."

Lloyd smiled hesitantly before tapping on his screen, bringing up my schedule for the day. "You don't normally need reminding, but you have a meeting this afternoon. You wanted to interview the temporary employee that would be filling in during my vacation next month."

"That's right. At one at Carl's?" If my schedule allowed, I preferred to do my interviewing out of the office. It allowed me to see how an applicant interacted with those around him, which was more important than his work history. And Carl's had a meatball sub that tasted just like home.

"Yes, I did want to confirm that you opened the listing to all types. Even omegas." I understood his hesitance. MattyCorp was one of two major businesses in the city that accepted omega, beta, and alpha applicants. Most only accepted the last two.

"Of course. Did we get many omega applicants?"

"None yet. I can widen the search, though, if today proves fruitless. There are some job boards that working omegas frequent."

Jobs like nannying and housework. Nothing wrong with either, but I hated imagining a life where their options were so limited. "Why don't you take a long lunch today, Lloyd? I know I haven't been the easiest wolf to work with these past few days."

Lloyd just shook his head and smiled. "Are you kidding me, sir?"

I understood what he meant. It wasn't me being narcissistic to see that I didn't act like most alphas. But that was because I had seen early on how brutal most alphas could be and vowed to never become that kind of monster. "Then why don't you just take a long lunch because? I can order you to, if you prefer?" I said the last part with a smile that Lloyd returned before accepting the offer.

I went to my office, watching through the glass wall as Lloyd called his partner, a beta as well, and gathered his things. He waved goodbye after checking in once more that I really was fine with him leaving. The moment the elevator doors shut behind him, I went to my computer, typing Wynn's name into the search engine as I'd done a hundred times since bumping into him again.

And like all the other times, there were pages of results from people named Wynn, but none of them matched the mysterious man from that night.

Not so mysterious. He fucks men for money. After so many years, it's safe to call that his career.

But as much as I was sure I knew who and what Wynn was, I couldn't stop the whisper in the back of my mind that said I had the situation wrong. Yeah, right. I *wanted* to have the situation wrong.

If I could find anything about the omega, then I could convince myself once and for all that I needed to get the young man out of my mind. He'd been so young the first time I'd seen him. A child. I'd had only concern for his situation back then, but now? I had more than concern.

"Where are you, Wynn?" I whispered while scrolling page after page.

There was a soft knock at my glass door, and I looked up, blinking several times at the sight before me.

The omega smiled small, tilting his head to the side in surprise. I looked back at the screen and then up at Wynn, standing outside my office. Was he some spirit I'd summoned?

That was ridiculous, but it didn't explain the itch at the back of my neck. I stood, watching Wynn's face on the other side of the glass and taking hesitant steps, expecting him to vanish like the figment of my imagination he probably was.

But, when I opened the door, he was still there: head slightly bowed, his hands clasped together in front of him, holding a file tight to his stomach. "Wynn?"

His cheeks went pink. "You do remember me. I swear I didn't know."

My neck still itched. Something wasn't quite right, but I was too elated to have this omega in front of me to care. "What didn't you know?" I asked, wondering if my voice had ever sounded so deep. My wolf wanted to impress this omega. Odd, since he didn't care what anyone else thought of him.

"That you were Magnus Gray. I saw this posting and it said it was open to omegas and I thought I would give it a try but I didn't know it was you and I can just go if you want me to." He spoke all in one breath, hurried words that mushed into and overlapped one another. "I know you...don't...just...the last time we—"

I settled my weight back on my heels in a position of disadvantage. Most alphas stood on the balls of their feet, always ready to burst into motion. But I'd been fighting those urges for so long that doing the opposite was slowly becoming my true nature. Except now, the moment I swayed back as I normally did, my wolf demanded I lean forward, to prepare for action. Did he sense danger? Was he preparing me to protect this omega?

The demure omega in front of me was a far cry from the confident wolf I'd witnessed in the bathroom. Was that the act? Or was this? Was it *all* an act? "You're here for the job?" I asked, reminding myself why he'd said he was here.

His golden eyes flared open. "The ad said..." He pulled out a sheet of paper from the folder. "Here, it said that omegas were welcome to apply."

"No, that's not what I mean. Omegas are welcome. Everyone is welcome at MattyCorp, but do you—do you *need* the job?"

He blinked at me, his expression confused. "Do I need it? Like, do I have a mate?"

"No—" I rubbed my mouth roughly to stop myself from continuing to say the wrong thing. I was coming off as a jerk. But I couldn't figure out why this omega who was obviously doing well selling himself for money would want to take up time sitting behind a desk for a fair yet reasonable salary. "Could I read the ad?" I asked as a horrible thought struck.

Wynn nodded, handing the paper over. He didn't move any closer, choosing instead to stretch his arm so that it reached close enough for me to grab. He was nervous and hesitant, probably because of how strange I was acting.

I skimmed the ad, seeing no language that could've been taken in a way that implied I was looking for a *special* assistant. I always forgot about the third type of posting that was available to omegas. "This is an office job, you understand," I said, wishing I could kick myself. Why was I pushing away the wolf I'd spent days obsessing over?

"Yeah, I sort of knew that once I read the heading that said 'Office Assistant needed.'"

Was he teasing me? Sure enough, a small smile flitted over his lips until it was like he realized and schooled his lips back into a natural resting position.

"Okay, fair enough," I said smiling in return. I liked it when his lips turned up in the corners. It made his face look less serious, less like he carried the weight of the world on his back. "Were you my one o'clock interview? I don't remember seeing your name on the list of applicants." And I knew that no omegas had applied.

Until now.

Calm down, Magnus. He could be woefully unqualified.

Somehow, I doubted that.

"I didn't have a way of contacting your office. I know the ad said to call first, but… I have a resume, and, well, it's pretty empty. But I know how to use the phone, and I've gotten experience with computers at the library."

The position of my assistant was quite a bit more than phones and computers, but I wasn't about to say anything to douse the excited gleam in Wynn's eye that first sparked as he spoke of his skills.

"That sounds good, but I do have an interview already scheduled today at one." I hated having to say as much, but it wouldn't really be fair of me to cancel with the wolf who had gone through the proper channels to schedule an interview for the omega standing in front of me. Even if the omega was currently looking at me like I alone ordered the sun to rise in the morning.

"Oh," Wynn said as what I said sunk in. "I'll go. I'm sorry that I—"

My hand shot out on instinct, grabbing his wrist. He tensed, probably because a strange alpha was wolfhandling him. "Don't go," I said, scrambling for my words to catch up with my actions. "Maybe you could help me for today. I like to see my applicants interacting in real-world situations. You could assist me, and I would pay your normal daily rate, of course."

He frowned. "My normal daily rate?"

I couldn't remember the last time I'd blushed, but it was like my body had saved it all up for now. They could probably see me from space. "I mean, I would pay you wages for the time you helped."

His eyes dropped, and I found I didn't like not being able to see them. He kept his gaze down. "You wouldn't have to pay me, Mr. Gray. I… I like being around you," he whispered sweetly.

And while I should have been over the moon at such a confession, I barely restrained my growl. The itch at my nape started up again. "I will pay you for your assistance," I said, walking to the corner to grab my jacket. "You'll be like a temporary employee," I added more for my benefit than his.

Because an employee meant hands-off.

***

Wynn had taken the bus to MattyCorp, so we shared a cab to Carl's. He admitted he'd never eaten there before, which made me oddly pleased that I would be able to be the one to introduce it to him.

Which was a little silly because he could not even like meatball subs.

"When the applicant gets there, I'll introduce you as Lloyd. If he gets the job, I'll tell the truth, and if he doesn't, then it won't matter. After I get a feel for the guy, I'll excuse myself. That's where you come in. Just talk to him. Try to strike up a conversation and then later, you can tell me how he was." I noticed I had a notification on my cell and opened it, reading the text from the applicant saying he would be less than five minutes late. "I'll be trusting you to tell me the truth," I said to Wynn, sliding my phone back in my pocket. "I know you came looking for a job and one day probably isn't what you were hoping for, but MattyCorp is a big company." I couldn't help but puffing with pride at that statement. "And I'm sure I can find a place for you after today."

Wynn smiled, but not in an excited, "I just got hired" kind of way. More like the same smile he'd been shooting me since first knocking on the glass door of my office. I looked closer at the omega beside me. His hands were folded tight, the folder still in his grip. He hadn't needed to call anyone to let them know where he was going. Did that mean he had a family that gave him free reign, or was he on his own?

Why did I feel like the tiny, covert glances he kept sending me were planned? If he really had spent the last ten years using his body for money, then he would be adept at controlling every action, using his every motion and gesture as a tool to manipulate his clients. The idea that he could possibly be utilizing the same techniques with me as he did with other men he'd eventually slept with made my hands clench.

But what right did I have to get angry at that? He was an omega who had learned how to navigate a world that wanted to keep his kind subservient. He wasn't covered in bruises, and he didn't flinch from my every word. Shouldn't I be pleased that he'd discovered a way to survive instead of angry at the how? It was a dangerous lifestyle, which was the reason I settled on why I was angry.

Maybe offering him a job would be good for him and me.

At Carl's, the waiter seated the two of us at a table with four chairs. I ordered us two meatball subs before pulling a chair out for Wynn, his eyes flashing a shocked gold as he took a seat. From my seat across from him, the sun shone through the window, lighting up the edges of his head and giving him a glow.

"How old are you?" I asked.

"Twenty-one," he replied softly.

"And you're sure you want a job at my company? Most omegas your age are looking for...something else."

"What should I be looking for, Mr. Gray?"

I squirmed, taking a long drink of my water. "Call me Magnus."

"Okay, what should I be looking for, Magnus?"

How did a question that was eight words long manage to instantly make my dick hard? I pulled out the collar of my shirt to let in a little cool air, catching Wynn's smirk. Was he doing this on purpose? Using that sultry tone and giving me coquettish looks that he likely practiced in a mirror? "I don't know. What sort of things do you like?"

He tapped a thin finger against his chin. There was a scar at his knuckle. I wanted to know how he got that scar, who gave it to him. Fuck, I wanted to know everything about this omega. What he'd been doing for the past ten years, what business he thought he had messing around with men older than myself when he was younger than I. He must be on his own because no alpha worth his howl would let him gallivant around like that, and any other sort of alpha would've beaten him down into a shell of who he'd been.

But Wynn didn't seem like a shell. He was an entire ocean, as mysterious as the seas were deep. And for some strange reason, I believed him to be just as dangerous.

Maybe to you and your work ethic.

The bell over the entrance rang, and we both looked. I knew the alpha walking in was my applicant right away. He was dressed smart in a blue striped suit and tie with no wrinkles. It was amazing how many young alphas thought they didn't have to dress for the job, but this one seemed to have gotten the memo, all the way down to his shiny loafers and black briefcase.

A guy like this would've been eaten up in the South Side. But here in downtown Wolf's Peak, he was in his element. His eyes found me, and he gave a polite wave before his gaze slid to Wynn.

"Thank you for meeting me here," I said, extending my hand. "This is my assistant, Lloyd."

Wynn raised his hand, and the alpha shook it gingerly, barely grabbing his fingertips and giving his hand a floppy wiggle.

Strike one.

"I knew you employed omegas, but I wasn't aware I'd be replacing one," the applicant said with a smile that didn't reach his eyes. "I have recently graduated from Wolf's Peak University with my degree in information technology and a minor in business." He said it as if that was going to make me leap up and exclaim he was clearly overqualified for a job that an omega had recently filled. The fact that an omega hadn't been in the position meant nothing to me. The applicant's attitude did.

"They have an amazing Marketing track at WPU," Wynn said softly, surprising us both but likely in different ways.

How did a man who claimed not to have access to a phone to set up an interview know anything about the marketing track at WPU?

The applicant recovered before I did. "You're right. One of the best." He gestured toward the chair beside Wynn. "Do you mind?"

Wynn waved him on, and the applicant sat down.

"My apologies for my lateness. I had a meeting run over."

I easily read between the lines. He'd had another interview and wanted me to know.

"Well, my boss prides himself in not just respecting his own time but the time of his employees, so you'll never have to worry about meetings running over with him," Wynn said. While I wondered how he knew, he *was* speaking the truth. He'd also taken the applicant's power play and transformed it into a selling point for me and my business.

I sat back and let him continue.

"The work he does at MattyCorp is not just a business. We make solutions. Does that sound like something you are interested in?" Again, I wondered how Wynn knew but was barely able to hide my grin.

The alpha applicant looked from Wynn to me and back. He clearly wasn't used to an omega taking point in a business meeting. That wasn't so bad, but how he responded to such a thing was what I wanted to see. "It is. I've heard amazing things about MattyCorp. For a company so young, you've made a name for yourself, outbidding and out-supplying every competitor."

"Thank you," Wynn replied solemnly. At that point I couldn't hide my laugh.

He was... refreshing. I'd asked him to put on this act, to help me figure out what sort of a man the applicant was, and he'd taken that in a delightfully playful yet appropriate direction. Except the applicant didn't know that, and now he was staring at me. "I need to use the restroom," I said, enacting the second stage of our plan.

But, when it came time to actually get up and walk away from the omega, I found that both myself and my wolf did not want to. I stood and lingered for so long Wynn sent me a questioning look. His glossy dark hair had fallen in his eyes in front, and I put my hand in my pocket to keep from brushing those hairs back and out of his way.

"I'll be right back," I said, taking the steps toward the hallway to the bathroom like I was walking through wet sand. I looked back, noticed neither was staring, and then ducked to the side behind a privacy screen that blocked the view into the kitchen. The cook noticed me, but I was a regular here, and this wasn't the first time I'd tested an employee.

He gave me a little salute and then pointed at the meatball sub on the cutting board in front of him, knowing that was what I came here for. My stomach rumbled.

But when I looked back at the table, the playful mood I'd left was gone. Wynn sat stock straight, bending like a reed in the wind away from the applicant. What had the alpha managed to say in the seconds since I'd left?

Wynn said something, but I couldn't read his lips, and the noise in the restaurant made it too hard for me to listen in. Whatever it was, the applicant stood, balled up his napkin and threw it at the table before grabbing his suitcase and nearly running out the door.

I hurried back, my hands out as if I was going to gather Wynn in my arms. I dropped them at the last second, taking the seat the applicant had left open. "What happened?"

"I don't know," Wynn replied, his eyes wide and round. "It was like you left, and he turned into a different person. He...propositioned me almost immediately."

I snarled, clenching my fists and whipping my head back to the door as if I was hoping he'd barge back in. He didn't, but our waiter did arrive then with the two subs we'd ordered. My stomach grumbled as the melted mozzarella, garlic, tomato, and Italian spices wafted into my face, not to mention the ever-present scent of freshly baked bread.

"This looks...amazing," Wynn said, looking over at me, all worry erased from his face.

"They are. I just wish you hadn't gone through what you did right before eating. That couldn't have helped your appeti—" The word died on its way out as I watched Wynn lift his sub, open his lips, and shove an entire quarter of the sandwich into his mouth.

He looked at me as if just noticing that I was there. "Sorry, what?" he asked with his mouth full. A speck of marinara sauce stuck to the corner of his lip.

I reached forward in a foggy haze, but regained my senses halfway through and grabbed a napkin, thrusting it toward him. "Nothing," I said with a smile.

I watched him take another satisfied, uncensored bite. He didn't try the ole "one nibble and I'm full" routine. He didn't even wait for me to start eating as most omegas had been trained to do. He just dug in. And I would say nothing to stop that.

We ate in silence. When the plates were empty, the waiter returned offering dessert. I'd been about to decline when Wynn asked to see the menu. We ended up getting two hot fudge sundaes, though he added caramel sauce to his. When the waiter brought them over, Wynn grabbed the salt shaker and sprinkled a tiny amount over his caramel. "I know the sodium is bad for water retention, but there's something about salty then sweet that really gets me going," Wynn explained.

Meanwhile, I tried not to concentrate on the noises of pleasure he made, or the way he swiped his finger around the inside of the bowl in an attempt to consume every last drop.

After a while I'd stopped eating my own food, choosing to watch him eat instead. I was beginning to see he did that with the same gusto he did everything else. *The same gusto he uses to sleep with alphas for money?*

That thought had less power over me than it had before. Maybe that was what he'd been, but he was something else now. I was sure of it. "Do you want to get out of here?" I asked the moment the words had formed.

Wynn stilled, and I panicked that I'd crossed the line, seeing something between us where there was nothing. "Back to the office?" he asked.

"Is that where you want to go?" I replied, finding it difficult to navigate this rocky terrain. If I came off too aggressive, it would make it seem like I was using my status as an alpha or his boss to order him around. "If it is, we can. I'll cut you a check for today, and we can talk to HR about open positions. But, if you wanted to go someplace else… We could walk around the park?" Suddenly, I felt fifteen again, asking my first omega if he wanted to hold hands at the dance. Admittedly, most of the time I should've spent perfecting my pick-up skills had been spent attempting to repel interested omegas. It wasn't until this moment that I regretted that.

"It is a nice day," Wynn said, wiping his mouth daintily with a napkin.

We decided to walk to Timber Greens from Carl's. The walk itself had been quiet. Wynn kept pace with me, which was only unusual because my entire life I'd been accused by alpha, beta, and omega alike for being too fast of a walker. I couldn't help it. When I had a goal and needed to get somewhere, I didn't see the point in dawdling. But Wynn didn't complain once. In fact there was a moment when I intentionally slowed down, thinking maybe he was too polite or shy to ask, and Wynn rushed ahead of me so far that I was the one skipping to catch up.

Which I did with a grin and rosy cheeks. I couldn't seem to stop smiling whenever I looked at the omega.

At the park, there were a few other people about. A group of omegas and a few betas circled around the playground as their pups played. Here, there were people in both their wolf and human form. We found an empty bench and watched a group of teens throwing Frisbees, taking turns between who was the human thrower and who got to be in their wolf form catching. Every once in awhile they would argue, claiming one group or the other had gotten more time catching. The arguments never progressed past typical alpha posturing.

We kept up small talk the entire time, with Wynn asking me about the company and why I was hiring an assistant. When his questions stopped, I asked my own, but that proved trickier than I realized.

"You went to Wolf's Peak University?" I asked.

"No, why would you think I did?"

"Because, earlier, at Carl's, you…"

Wynn just blinked in that mysterious way.

"Do you live near here?" I asked, thinking surely this

was a safer topic.

"No," Wynn replied, and it took me a few seconds to realize that was all he was going to say about the matter.

Then, suddenly, he stiffened. My body mirrored his, preparing for a threat that he needed protecting from. I followed the line of his sight and saw the cause immediately. An alpha walked down the main path of the park, holding a leash in his hand. He had the body language of a self-possessed man without a care in the world. The animal at the end of his leash was a wolf wearing a diamond-studded collar.

One of the last truly heinous laws to be passed stated that it was legal for an alpha to *collar* their omegas, which meant an alpha could demand their omega remain in wolf form as a type of punishment. Omegas had been rallying against such cruelty, saying it was demeaning and inhumane. I agreed, but the general voting population did not. Not surprising when the voting process was evaluated. An alpha vote was weighted and worth the same as two omega votes.

The closer the alpha and his omega pet grew, the stiffer Wynn became until the alpha passed right in front of us. His eyes glazed over Wynn, landing on me and giving me a nod I did not return. I feared at this point a light breeze would shatter Wynn into a thousand pieces. He didn't speak, didn't breathe as he watched the pair continue to walk by. Then, out of nowhere, he bent down, grabbed a rock the size of a penny, and chucked it. It soared through the air, pinging against the back of the alpha's head. He grabbed his hair, rubbing the spot and turning our way, his eyes immediately finding Wynn.

"Run!" Wynn grabbed my hand and tugged me to my feet, and we took off the opposite direction, a stream of curse words fading behind us. At some point during our escape, Wynn threw his head back, the sun making his skin glow as his red lips parted and the most delightful tinkling laugh escaped.

44

When we were almost to the other side of the park, I slowed us down. The alpha had never even attempted to chase us. We stopped under a tree, panting as we caught our breaths—a job made more difficult by the wheezing laughs that still bubbled out of us both.

"That was very dangerous," I said through pants.

"I knew..." Wynn took several deep breaths. "...I could outrun him."

Another thing that set Wynn apart from any other omega I'd ever met. Outside of the bedroom, they didn't boast of their physical prowess, especially in comparison to an alpha.

As the thrill of the chase wore off, something else settled between us. Something unspoken but alluring. I couldn't take my eyes off him, unwilling to miss a single blink. Wynn, however, began looking everywhere but at me. Was I making him nervous? Or was he playing the part of bashful omega? I took a step, bringing our bodies closer together as I stared at his lips. He licked them, and I stifled a groan, but my body had a mind of its own, and there was nothing I could do about the pheromones pouring out of me or the cock rapidly swelling and pressing against my zipper. Wynn stumbled, backing up against the trunk of the willow tree, its drooping branches shielded us from most eyes.

I claimed the space he'd given up, one hand rising to the space on the trunk just above and to the right of his head. "I'm sorry. This is so inappropriate," I murmured, our faces so close together I hardly needed to speak for him to hear me.

"You're not like other alphas," Wynn replied, but he didn't say it like the fact made him happy.

Still, he didn't turn his face as I brought our mouths even closer together. "I was going to say the same about you."

"I'm not like other alphas?" Wynn breathed.

My laugh was more like a low rumble. My other hand

went to the hair that had again fallen forward into his eyes, and I brushed the strands to the side. "I'm glad you're different," I said before closing the remaining gap. The first touch of our lips together snapped like static electricity. The air around us seemed to crackle from it, but I didn't care as I deepened the kiss, probing gently forward with my lips and tongue while I cupped his face, then his nape, then further down to his waist.

My tongue was inside of his mouth, exploring the warm depths as I got my first taste of him. Just like with his scent, the taste of him was light but alluring, reminding me of peaches.

Then, out of nowhere, he growled. I worried that I'd misstepped, pushed him further than he wanted, except in the next moment he spun us around. Now my back was against the trunk as he brought his leg up like a barrier on one side that caged me to him. Before I could moan or growl or do anything, he pulled back, his eyes wide and his expression one of shock.

"I'm s-s-sorry," he stammered, reaching his fingertips to his lips as he did. "I don't know what...that was, I'm sorry."

"Hey." I reached for his wrist, but he dodged to the side. I took the hint, shoving my hands in my pockets, but moving to at least slow down his escape. "It's okay. I didn't mind."

"Are you sure?" he asked like he could hardly believe it.

At that point I was sure of two things. No omega had ever kissed me like that. And no kiss would ever compare to the one I'd just experienced. My heart pounded as my wolf howled. He loved the push and pull of power, of not just dominating another man, but dominating a man that was choosing me. He wasn't here because he felt forced or because he had no other choice. "I'm positive."

In the next second, a flash of light sparked overhead, and the skies opened up. I wasn't sure when the dark clouds had moved in, but the static electricity I'd felt around us made more sense the moment another bolt of lightning flashed directly above our heads, followed by a booming rumble of thunder.

Wynn shrieked, the most stereotypically omega thing I'd seen him do yet.

"I live near here," I said, trying not to sound like I'd planned this. I reached out my hand as the rain really began to pour.

Wynn studied my face, likely trying to decide if I'd somehow arranged for the summer thunderstorm. But, after a moment he grabbed my hand, and we kept running out of the park and down the two blocks to my high-rise apartment building.

I waved to Stu, the beta security guard at the front desk. Now that he'd seen me with Wynn, he would remember his face. Stu was amazing like that. And he took care of his omega brother's two children after he'd died four years ago.

We took the elevator up to the penthouse floor, an action that required a code. I made no motion to hide the four-digit number. When the doors opened to my apartment, I gestured for Wynn to enter first. We stopped by the closest bathroom, snagging two towels. I draped mine around my shoulders and motioned for Wynn to stand still as I dried his hair, but he tugged the towel from me while I tried to not let my disappointment show.

My wolf paced, unhappy that there was any distance between us, but what did the beast expect after a day—not even a day—hours with each other? An offer of mating?

My wolf shrugged as if to say, *Why not?*

Meanwhile, Wynn dried his own hair while walking around the open layout of the penthouse. "How much of this do you own?" he asked.

"The whole thing," I said with a pride I didn't normally feel. I tended to avoid talking about my real estate and other possessions, but at this point I was pretty sure Wynn wasn't after me for my money. He wouldn't have strayed so far out of the omega dating playbook if he had been.

"The whole floor?" he asked.

I smiled a little, glad for the first time that I'd made the early investment. "The whole building."

Wynn's mouth dropped open as he looked out at the west wall made entirely of glass that was actually bullet-resistant, transparent armor. The whole city sprawled out below us, and for a few seconds, we stood there, staring at the rain soaking the city. "I'm nervous," Wynn admitted as I stepped up behind him.

I tugged the towel from his hands, draping it over the chair before settling my hands on his hips. "Do you want me to stop?" I asked, praying and hoping I knew the answer to that question.

"The fact that you even asked that is amazing. How are you... so... you?"

At first, I thought he'd been thrown off simply by how not like a typical alpha I was, but now it felt like more than that. Like he'd heard things about me that were proving not to be true. But then, he turned in my arms, canting his head back and offering his lips to me so sweetly that I forgot about anything that wasn't this. That wasn't us.

I held him tightly with a hand at the back of his head and one at his hip as we continued the kiss that we started in the park. He let me take the lead, but it didn't feel like a surrender, more like I'd earned the right to govern our interaction.

Though the kiss began sweeter, it quickly heated up. My hands went to his ass, lifting him smoothly as he wrapped his legs around my middle. Our dicks rubbed against each other over our clothing. "I'm not... near a heat," he said between kisses.

He was telling me that our sex wouldn't result in an unwanted pregnancy, but I didn't know if there was anything that could happen between us that was unwanted. I growled into his mouth on the next kiss, giving him no choice but to swallow the sound as I carried him to the master bedroom. The wall of windows continued in this room, and I pressed the shade button that tinted the glass so that we could see out but no one could see in.

He gave the windows a double-take, but I needed his lips and wanted his eyes on me, so I hooked my index under his chin, bringing his face back my way. "We don't have to do anything," I told him. Though I whispered, my voice still felt too loud. Like it would break whatever spell had brought this amazing man into my life.

"I know," Wynn replied before pulling his shirt off. He wasn't quite slim, but wasn't quite muscular either. He had definition in his abs and chest. Not so unusual for an omega, but adding it to everything else that was unique about him, he became the total, unexpected package.

"I mean it. We can just keep kissing or cuddle or—"

He silenced me with a well-timed pounce. My back hit the mattress, and he landed on top of me, stretching his arms up over his head as if he pounced on alphas for a living. I gripped his hips and spun, stopping when he was tucked under me. I liked the way that felt.

"Hold on. I don't want you to hurt, Wynn. Let me get you ready." I undid his pants, slipping them down and tossing them to the side of the bed, my clothes following quickly behind.

"I've been ready since we met in the bathroom," he blurted, and I got the idea he hadn't meant to say as much. I also got the idea that he wasn't used to saying things he didn't completely mean to. He continued in a softer, almost contrite voice. "I couldn't stop thinking about you. About this."

That brought up questions of how much of a coincidence this morning really was, but I wasn't stupid enough to stop what we were doing so we could hash it out. So what if he looked me up? I'd done the same but had just been less successful. "I know what you mean. I felt so stupid after. I'm sorry about how I acted."

That got a smile out of him. "Don't tell me you're

sorry," he said, leaning back and lifting his ass so that I had better access to his sweet hole. "Show me."

I reached to the nightstand for the lube I used for my personal moments. I knew what I would be imagining for every personal moment from this day on: the scene in front of me right now.

Wynn stared at my erect cock, licking his lips. He had this way of making me feel pride in areas that I'd previously tried to diminish or hide. When he stared at me like that, I wanted to grab my cock and put it on display for his viewing pleasure. I'd do anything for his pleasure. And right now, my omega wanted me to fuck him.

I lubed up, saving some to lather around his greedy hole. Sure enough, he'd been telling the truth when he said he was ready. I dropped down, placing the head of my dick against his entrance and pausing, loving the way his pucker fluttered against me.

"Did you think of me after that night?" I asked him, pushing just the tip against the tight ring of muscles.

"Yes," he hissed.

"And you touched yourself while you thought of me? Here?" I punctuated my question with another forward thrust.

His hips shot off the bed, and he wailed, the noise turning into a *yes* halfway through.

"I did the same." Every night. Sometimes twice a night.

"I thought about what would have happened if I'd grabbed you, made you stay," Wynn said, the words spilling from his lips almost as if he'd drank truth serum and the effects were just starting to kick in. "I imagined guiding us into the stall, getting on my knees, and sucking your cock. I thought about you bending me over and taking what you wanted. But it would have been what I wanted too."

As he spoke his fantasies, I was living mine. I pushed the rest of the way, pressing our groins together and letting him adjust to my size before beginning to thrust. "In the bathroom, omega? What if people heard us?"

"I thought about that as well," he whispered. "I was stuffed full and unable to control my moans, forcing you to clamp your hand over my mouth. But I was still too noisy, so you gave me something else to suck on."

"Like this?" I asked, thrusting my middle and index finger through his lips. His mouth clamped down, and his cheeks hollowed as a noise that was the mix between a growl and a whimper rumbled out of him.

He continued sucking my fingers, showing me what he would do to my dick later as I pumped into him. My ass muscles flexed with every forward thrust, and his inner muscles clenched around me, unhappy about letting me go.

Then his mouth opened. I moved my hand so as not to block the most glorious howl. My omega's dick spurted creamy fluid as he came, bringing his mouth to my chest, my arm, whatever parts of me he could reach as he nibbled and licked through his orgasm.

I wanted to fuck him forever, but it had been so long and he'd come so thoroughly that I wasn't long behind him. As my balls tightened to my body and my thrusts grew erratic, I wished he was near his heat. Fuck that. I wished he was *in heat* so that my knot would swell inside him and lock our bodies together.

But, when my orgasm began crashing through my body, I barely had my wits about me enough to keep my upper half held above him. I didn't want to crush him, though, so I locked my elbows as my hips slammed forward like a stuttering jackhammer. I roared and bent my arms, unthinking, as I clamped my teeth on the spot where his neck and shoulder met. I didn't break skin, but held on tight enough so that he would remain beneath me as I spilled my seed inside.

I lifted, suddenly afraid that I'd gone too far, too fast, too much, but the satisfied look Wynn gave me calmed my worries. I kissed him softly on the lips before sliding out and lowering to the side of him.

"You're okay? I didn't hurt you?"

I couldn't see the front of his face, but saw the side of his cheek move in a smile. "No, you didn't hurt me. I don't need to wait for the rain to stop, though, if you... if you want me to go?"

I frowned, glad he couldn't see my expression. "Do you need to go? If you don't have anything to go to, you could stay. We could order dinner?"

He sighed, and the sound was so wistful I was sure he was going to refuse. "That sounds great."

He settled more deeply into the mattress and tucked his ass back into me as we spooned and watched the rain fall.

CHAPTER FIVE
Wynn

To pass the time, I counted each breath while trying to reconcile the alpha who was my target with the alpha slowly falling asleep beside me.

I'm glad you're different.

Why would an alpha hell-bent on oppressing omegas and keeping their location trackable at all times say something like that?

Unless...

He *wasn't* hell-bent on oppressing omegas.

And he *didn't* want them trackable at all times.

But if that was the case, then Taft wouldn't have sent me his file. He wouldn't have accepted the job. He wouldn't have assigned me, the one omega on my team that was a stickler about the why. I wanted to know what my targets did, often delving deeper than my other teammates would dare. These alphas that we eliminated had done horrible things, after all, and seeing the aftermath of those crimes was always hard to stomach. That was the point. But, for me to be effective, to act without mercy or hesitation, I had to *know*.

After about an hour of counting breaths, I dared to open an eye. I was lucky to be getting this chance. Dinner had turned into more sex—just as amazing as the first—and then Magnus had shyly asked if I could stay the night. I would've been flattered if that hadn't been the exact thing I'd been angling for the entire day. I hadn't expected the day to go so easily, had only planned on laying the foundation of getting into his home at some point later on. But we'd gone from his office, to the cab, to the restaurant and then park so quickly and seamlessly that I had to remind myself that this wasn't a date. I wasn't a timid omega looking for a job, and he wasn't the magnanimous alpha he portrayed himself to be.

It was an act.

It had to be.

I didn't know the purpose behind such a play, but wasn't I here to get information?

I wiggled, as if caught up in a dream and waited for any response. The arm Magnus had wrapped around me tightened in a hugging motion before relaxing, resting gently at my hip. Sleeping with him had been a mistake. Not because I hadn't wanted it or anything like that, but because laying in his arms felt more comfortable, more *right* than it should have.

Maybe I was losing my touch, losing my drive.

I thought of the anger that had driven me as a child. The utter injustice that I felt being pushed, pulled, flayed apart against my will. Who would save the omegas like me, seven years old, facing their first of a lifetime of trials they would endure simply for being born an omega?

Me. I would.

I just needed to find the evidence. Find the files I was looking for—and if he happened to have other incriminating evidence I would find that too, commit it all to memory and remember this moment for the next time an alpha didn't act like the complete monster he was inside.

Magnus pulled his arm free, turning over on his other side with a sigh. Instantly, the parts of me that had pressed against him felt cold. *This* was what I needed to concentrate on.

Before I lost my nerve, I slipped my feet on the ground. The carpet was soft beneath my feet, plush like a field of new grass not yet roughened by wind or wear. I thought of the old threadbare carpet of my early childhood years. Stained and fraying in places. I'd learned to crawl, learned to walk on that while this guy got to walk on clouds.

I let that annoyance propel me forward, walking in slow spurts through his room, looking for anything obvious and out in the open while also making sure I wasn't tripping any motion sensors. I didn't think of Magnus as the type to arm his home like a fortress. He hadn't even bothered to hide his floor code, seven-four-nine-eight. But he had to have some sort of security. Otherwise, whoever had hired us would've gotten the files they needed on their own.

So I was careful as I padded out of the main bedroom and through the living room. The windows out here remained untinted, and I gave the night view a quick glance. So many people living so close together, so many suffering—like that omega I'd seen this afternoon in the park, forced into his wolf form by a master that couldn't control him otherwise.

Magnus hadn't had a problem with my swift justice in that situation. Only that it could bring danger closer to me.

Just because he isn't actively beating omegas every second you look at him doesn't mean he doesn't deserve this. As I tried to work out the double and triple negatives in my thought, I entered into a room that I'd thought was a spare bedroom. There was a desk with a desk lamp, but nothing else on the surface. The filing cabinet looked promising, as well as the computer tower I spotted under the desk.

I kept the light off and sat on the large, cushioned office chair trying to figure out where he kept the monitor that went with the tower. I leaned my forearm on the desktop as I reached for one of the drawers. The drawer was locked, but leaning on the desktop had set off a sensor that opened a flap on the far edge of the desk. A thin touchscreen monitor whirred up into place, the screen lighting up like a beacon. Thankfully, it faced away from the door, but I would need to be fast anyway. I didn't have any information on what type of a sleeper Magnus was. He could have the bladder of a peanut.

I doubted it since he had the dick of a god.

I blushed as my fingers flew over the screen, opening files at random while I thought about the noises Magnus had wrenched from me the day before. We were required by the OAC to keep a healthy, regular sexual lifestyle. Betas and sometimes alphas were brought in regularly to assist us in that area—we called them comfort monitors—and our heats were charted carefully. It would do no good to be out on a mission, gearing up to eliminate a target, only to fall into a heat. Barring any spontaneous heat, I was good for a few more weeks. And if I did spontaneously go into heat, I had just the blockers necessary to get me to a safe location. Highly illegal blockers, but I wasn't going to flash them around. My stomach flipped as an image popped in my mind, unbidden and unwanted, but impossible for me to not dwell on now that it had formed. In my mind, I was wanton, needy and begging for my alpha's dick. Sex while in heat was always a thousand times better—last night's escapades excluded. If Magnus had made me howl like that between cycles, what could he make me do when he gave me his knot?

When? That was a dangerous slip, implying I had more of a future than was possible. I turned my full attention back to the screen, knowing now more than ever that I needed to hurry and find the information, confirm it with the client and then finish the job. After, I'd request a week and book every single comfort monitor that was willing and available. That would get whatever this was out of my system.

Except the thought of doing just that made me feel like I'd eaten a pile of slugs, and they were now slithering around my stomach in slimy protest.

I spotted a folder labeled Home and tapped it. The file was full of pictures: smiling faces of alphas, betas, and omegas of different ages. Some featured the groups staring at the camera, while others were more candid shots. Magnus was in a few of them, but he looked different. His face was more carefree, and his clothes were much more dressed down than anything I'd seen him wear since.

The file I'd been given didn't have much on his life before moving to downtown Wolf's Peak. The client hadn't seemed all that worried with who he'd been, just with who he was. This information could be useful. At least, that was what I told myself as I scrolled through them. Hundreds of images, all from the same dingy, urban locations. Streets lined with litter, buildings decorated with graffiti and broken windows, a far cry from the grassy carpet and bulletproof windows. As I scrolled, the pictures got older. Magnus grew younger before my eyes. He also smiled less. That was, until I found one of him with his arm around a boy. I was sure of two things: the boy was related to him in some way and was likely an omega. A delicate one at that. The boy reminded me of River with his smaller stature and perfect curls.

But he wasn't in any of the newer pictures.

"You'll need a password to get into any of the juicy stuff," Magnus said, making me gasp and leap to my feet.

I couldn't recall the last time someone had snuck up on me. "Magnus, I—"

"Please don't," Magnus replied, sounding more weary than angry. "I don't want to hear anything else. I knew what you were, but I thought you were different."

He knew what I was? I doubted that. But, he thought he knew what I was, and I was curious.

"It's just pictures, Magnus. I'm looking at pictures," I said, spinning the screen his way.

He stood there for a moment, his hands clenched into fists at the ends of arms that were slightly splayed, so that he took up the space of the doorway. His hair brushed against the upper sill. He was shirtless, unconcerned by the expanse of toned flesh on display. His sweats sat low on his hips, and since I knew he hadn't gone to bed with them on, I figured he'd gotten up, saw me gone, and hurried them on. "You got up in the middle of the night, snuck out of my bed, and crept down the hallway to look at pictures? Wynn, I'm not stupid. I didn't say this before because I didn't want to embarrass you, but I *know* what you are."

Again, I doubted that. I looked around my person for a weapon anyway. My dumb ass had come into this office unarmed, assuming that Magnus would be too satisfied and exhausted from our sex earlier to wake. How had I gone from being warm in his arms to looking for something to harm him with?

It was the way my job went sometimes—though Magnus was the first target I'd ever had intercourse with. I'd fondled and played around if it meant lulling my target into a false sense of security, but I drew the line at penetration. And now look what happened. I'd been caught snooping, a rookie mistake. Nolan would never let me hear the fucking end of it. That was, if I got out of here alive. Which was the other weird thing. Magnus didn't look like he was raging. He just looked... hurt.

"What am I, Magnus?" I whispered.

"Why do I have to say it? What good will it do?" Magnus asked, rubbing his face roughly.

"Because I want to know. You say you know what I am. Tell me, what am I?"

"A hooker, okay? You're a hooker. And I know because I saw you about ten years ago. I remembered that moment. I was in my first years in the city. You were *so young*. I tried to save you because I thought you were being forced to dote on the old alpha you were with, but you both made it clear that you were right where you wanted to be. I left that bar, but you never left my mind, until you popped out of nowhere a few days ago. I didn't recognize you at first, but when I did—"

"You rejected me." *But still made sure I had a safe way home.*

Magnus opened his mouth like he was going to contradict me but sighed instead. "I should have stuck with my original decision."

He would have too, if it hadn't still been my job to get closer to him. He didn't know what I was, not really. But this wasn't any less dangerous. While the missions I'd been on when I was as young as ten had been for training purposes, the targets were still very real. I tried to recall the exact one he was talking about. A bar, an older alpha, a scuffle that I would've scrambled to resolve so it didn't derail the night from me getting the info I needed.

The blood drained from my face.

"I see you're remembering," Magnus quipped, his eyes narrowing.

I was, just not what he thought.

"That was a very long time ago. You have a good memory." I could barely get the words out.

He winced. I'd all but confirmed his accusation. "I do. I also remember looking up that older alpha after the fact, I don't know what I thought I would do. Beat him up, maybe. I was young. But he'd disappeared. No one ever heard from him again."

My heart pounded as my body tensed, preparing for action. Magnus didn't know what he knew, but that didn't matter. I remembered that alpha now, and the information I was looking for. Rumors had swirled around him for years that young omegas went missing when he was around. Not just the poor or the sex workers. Omegas from affluent families were disappearing. While the alpha's number was up, the higher-ups had worried that he'd had an omega prisoner at that exact time and that killing the alpha without getting his location would basically be the same as killing his omega prisoner.

Not only had the sordid details of that case stuck in my brain, but I remembered it for another reason. It had been my first field mission. And I'd successfully figured out the location of his torture dungeon, relaying the information to the extraction teams while the omega assigned to his extermination took over. I'd been an instant success and had enjoyed months of praise.

And the alpha had never been heard from, as easy to hide as he was for the rest of the world to forget.

The rest of the world minus myself and the alpha currently blocking my only exit. He had no idea how dangerous his information was, that even putting me in the same room as the missing alpha would be enough to compromise my entire position at the OAC. If the police questioned him about it, if some eager, rookie cop cracked open the cold case, he could follow the breadcrumbs. Receipts would put the alpha at the bar. While it had been part of my training to avoid showing the camera my face, surveillance of the night would show a scuffle, and Magnus could point his finger right at me.

I spotted a silver letter opener sitting in the top drawer of the desk that must've jarred a centimeter open when I stood.

"Wynn, you're shaking. I'm not going to hurt you, okay? I just—I want you to leave."

He stepped to the side.

I blinked. My body had been so ready for a fight that it took me a moment to readjust my thinking from how best to combat him to simply walking out.

He was going to let me walk out?

Magnus snarled. "Jesus, I hate that you look like that! Like you're shocked that I'm not beating you or something. Have you been paying attention to anything I've said? I know this day was a farce. You were only trying to get more information on me, more points of manipulation to help you secure me as a client. But I won't be one alpha of many. I may not be like the alphas you know, but I still don't share. And you're clearly attached to your lifestyle, so I think it is best for you to grab your things and leave. I'll wait for you in the kitchen." At that, he turned and disappeared, leaving me alone again in his office.

I looked down at his computer, I couldn't find anything in the seconds I probably had to vacate. But that wasn't what weighed on me. I wasn't even mad—yet—that I'd failed. And, at that second, I wasn't scared that Magnus would tattle.

I was just sad.

CHAPTER SIX
Wynn

Somewhere along the journey from Magnus's apartment to OAC headquarters, my sadness reverted back to panic. This could be the end of my lifestyle. The end of doing good, of making a difference. I knew I'd been going through some hiccups, but that hadn't meant I'd wanted to be stripped completely of power. And if I wasn't a member of the Omega Assassins Club, then what was I?

Just another frightened omega. I didn't bother returning to my barracks. It was past dawn when the taxi dropped me off at the gated entrance, and I walked straight into Taft's office.

He was there, despite the early morning hour, dressed in a black three-piece suit with a satin vest. The familiar sight helped soothe my nerves a little, if only in that it reminded me that some things were still operating normally. I stood in the doorway, unnoticed still as he drank his coffee and studied the file on his desk intently.

"Can I help you, agent?" Taft asked without looking up.

So much for being unnoticed. I shuffled in, shutting his door behind me. "Sir... I..." I couldn't bring myself to say the words that would rip me from the only life I'd ever chosen.

"Wynn? What happened?"

My gaze had dropped to the floor so I only heard Taft stand and walk toward me. I felt the heat of his body less than a foot away and realized with horror that tears were falling from my eyes with each blink.

"Are you hurt? Did the target do something?" He growled and gripped my arms above the elbows, jerking me so roughly I gasped.

He ripped the collar of my shirt down, revealing the bruise-like mark at the base of my neck. "He bit you. A mating mark? Fucking piece of shit. Did he rape you? Wynn, talk to me." The last bit was said more sharply than the rest, an order, not a request.

I blinked rapidly, trying to force the rest of my tears out before looking at him. "He didn't r-rape me. I slept with him, consensually."

The grip he had on my arms tightened. "But you don't… you aren't like the other agents."

How far we went with a target was up to the agent on the mission. Theoretically, I could've fucked every alpha I'd ever dispatched. But it had always been a limit of mine. Until now.

The worst part was that now I was out of Magnus's vicinity, I couldn't even remember why.

"I shouldn't have assigned you the case. You get too attached. You do more research on each target than any other agent in this organization. This was my fault, Wynn. You're too kind."

I frowned. It felt good that he wasn't blaming me, but calling me kind felt like a stretch. On a mission I was cold and calculated. "River is the kind one," I said to get the attention off of me.

"You wouldn't say that if you were on one of the crews assigned to cleanup his aftermath," he said darkly. "Come, sit."

I let him guide me to the chairs by his desk. Like

63

before, he chose to grab a chair and sit beside me rather than have the desk between us. Unlike before, he sat much closer. So close, our knees bumped together. He slipped one of his between mine.

"I've been watching you since my first day here, Wynn, and I have never seen someone make you cry. And the fact that you're here now tells me you either finished the mission and couldn't stomach calling it in, or…"

I tried to grasp onto the tiny fluttering of pride I felt when Taft assumed I could possibly be finished. He had that much faith in my abilities. "I can't do it," I whispered, watching the pride float away like butterflies.

"Because you fucked?" he snapped. The way he spoke about what Magnus and I had done made it seem like something dirty. But it hadn't been. It had been intimate, consensual, and loving.

That was the problem.

"Maybe there's been a mistake?" I asked, lifting my face toward his. "Maybe the client was confused about him, Taft. Magnus isn't—"

"Magnus? You're on a first-name basis with your target? Or have you forgotten that's what he is?" He stood with a growl, went around to the other side of his desk, and pulled out a file. "I didn't want to show you these because I know how you internalize the horrors. You left with a *mating mark*," he snarled. "The rest of these omegas weren't so lucky."

He slapped the first eight-by-ten color photo on the desktop. It was a crime scene. Evidence markers surrounded a rumpled heap that must've once been a person. A pool of blood had gathered around the body, but his face was unrecognizable because he was so badly beaten. That picture was covered by another, an omega with dark brown hair like mine, sitting hunched in a chair. The only thing keeping his lifeless form from slumping to the ground were the chains wrapped around his naked torso.

"My target did this?" I asked, my voice as hollow as I felt.

"These may not be his photos, but I'm sure if we dug far enough into his past, we'd find photos just like this."

I'd started to shake my head no, but stopped. How could I be sure? He was an alpha, a powerful one. And what alpha had climbed to power without stepping on a few little guys along the way? "I don't know. I couldn't find anything in his home. And he was so nice. I started to worry." I looked back over. "If I just had some proof. This is why I hate these kinds of missions. Why did you assign this one to me?" My whine grated on my own ears, but Taft only smiled, grabbing my hand and holding it in the space between our bodies.

"I gave it to you because I knew you could handle it. And because I thought you'd find the information easily. Wynn, you are my best agent, better than any member on your team."

I tugged my hand away. This wasn't like anything he'd said to me before. He didn't encourage competition between the agents, saying such childish urges put the agents and organization at risk.

"But I'm beginning to doubt that decision. The fact that you slept with your target makes me think I should reassign the case to another omega."

"What?" I snapped, my heart pounding. Another omega? One that wouldn't care what Magnus had done, who would only care about getting the job done has efficiently as possible? "If you did that, my team would never respect me. They'd think I can't get the job done."

Taft studied my face before frowning. "Why do I think you're more upset about another omega around this alpha than you are at the possibility of losing your peers' respect?"

"I've never been pulled off a mission before," I replied, getting to my feet. "For you to do that now would get gossip going. Then what happens the next time my team has a group job? They won't think I can cut it." That was partly true. Van, River and Zed would understand. But Nolan would never let me hear the end of it. "Sleeping with him was a mistake." At least that I could say with one hundred percent honesty. "I won't make that mistake again. Please, if you take me off now, it will be like he won. I'll have lost the motivation that drives me. I know I won't come out the same, I just know it."

"Sh, sh," Taft soothed, getting to his feet as well. He wrapped his thick arms around me, and while I didn't lean into the embrace, I didn't pull away either. I stood there, inhaling the scent of coffee and alpha male. "I have faith in you. I wouldn't have assigned you if I didn't think you could do it. Go back to him, get the chip schematics and then make it look like an accident or a mugging. But Wynn, if I find out you fucked him again, I will take you off the case. Do you understand?"

I sniffed, leftover from when I'd been crying. A fact I still couldn't believe. I didn't even remember the last time I'd cried. Until now. And it had been over a fucking alpha. "I understand," I replied, nodding. I pulled away, thinking there was no more to say, but Taft held on. I turned my face upwards, the question in my expression.

"I don't think you realize how important you are, to the OAC and... to me." He lowered his face and I realized a second before that he was going to kiss me.

My body reacted instantly, ducking out of his hold and spinning around so that I stood behind the chair, holding it between us like a shield. "What are you doing?" I snarled, wondering what was so different between kissing Taft and Magnus. They were both alphas. One was considerably less evil than the other. Maybe that was my problem. I'd been around darkness for so long. I didn't feel comfortable around anything else.

"Wynn, relax. I was just trying to comfort you. I didn't realize you were so uptight, though. I'll make a note of that moving forward."

His answer didn't feel right. But nothing had felt right to me. Not since meeting Magnus. That fucking alpha had wormed his way inside of my head, twisting around my every nerve ending and tainting my thoughts with him. I deflated, the tension pouring out of my body as my shoulders slumped. "I'm sorry. I'm... I need a shower."

Taft stepped closer, pulling the chair from my grasp and setting it back on the carpet. "You don't need to apologize. Take the rest of the day, I want you to go to medical and get tested—"

"I'm not—"

"I know you aren't near your heat cycle, but do your old director a favor and get checked over anyway. I'll set up a meeting with the counselor as well, in case you have any...lingering feelings."

I shook my head. "I really want to get back on the case before that." And I hated talking to the shrinks. They always wanted to ask why and how.

Taft stared at me, but after a moment he sighed. "I find it hard to say no to you. Okay, no counselor, but you will talk to them during debriefing after your meeting. I'll make sure Remington knows."

I smiled, already feeling lighter that I wouldn't have to go sit and talk about my feelings. "Thank you. And thank you for today. I... don't know..."

"It's fine. Just don't cry over another alpha again. I don't think I can take it."

I cocked my head to the side, my mouth opening to ask why, but he laughed suddenly. "Get out of here. You're bringing the emotional out of us both."

CHAPTER SEVEN
Magnus

I growled at my phone as it trilled, in no mood to answer any of Lloyd's questions. I'd taken the day before off, giving the excuse that I was sick. Really, I'd just known it would've been impossible to be in the office without thinking of the time Wynn had spent there. Which would have put me in such a foul mood, no one would have been safe.

That continued to today, Friday. My employees played hooky on Fridays all the time. They thought I didn't notice how they always seemed to get sick or lose family members on Thursday nights, but I did. I was just too nice of an alpha to admit it. And now, I couldn't take two consecutive weekdays off for the first time in years?

I got to my feet, spinning in a circle to find a more comfortable position. I'd woken that morning in my wolf form and had never bothered shifting back. When I'd been younger, I'd reverted to my wolf form whenever I was scared or sad. After Matty had been killed, I'd stayed that way for over a week. It was one thing to be forced into your wolf form by someone exerting control over you and quite another to choose that form for the solace it provided.

I'd risen, managed to open the fridge with my muzzle, and pulled out a pack of T-bone steaks I'd gotten from the butcher's. At the time, I'd planned on grilling them. But I'd spent the day on the deck off the living room, lazily gnawing on the meat until there were only bones left.

Except, about twenty minutes ago, my phone had begun to buzz and refused to stop.

I just wanted to wallow. I didn't want to worry about schooling my reactions and not hurting anyone's feelings. But when I heard someone knocking at the locked door to the emergency stairs, I knew that was going to be an impossible dream. I shifted, called out for whoever it was to wait a moment, and went into my room, grabbing the first pair of pants I saw.

They were the same sweats I'd been wearing when *Wynn* had shown his true nature. My jaw was so tense it ached.

I didn't know what was wrong with me, what had come over me. Was it because I hadn't opened my heart in so long? Was that why this betrayal hurt so deeply? In a very small amount of time, Wynn had become extremely special to me. And then he'd shown his true colors. I was just another mark to him. I'd caught him snooping, looking for information to further lure me into his trap.

After he'd left, I'd gone to the computer. Seeing the picture of me and Matty had been like the final nail in my coffin.

And then there was the equally confusing fact that I was upset Wynn had left like I'd asked him to. I'd watched him go, shaking like a leaf. He'd been terrified of me. I thought that was what had hurt the most. If Wynn still thought me capable of harming him, then he didn't know me at all.

"What is it?" I asked, yanking the service door open.

Stu stood on the other side, his face red and worried. "Sir, I am sorry, but you locked the elevator from reaching this floor—"

"I thought that would be a hint that I don't want to be disturbed," I sighed back and immediately felt like a dick. "I'm sorry, Stu. I am not myself. I need a long weekend and— What?"

"It's just—that omega from before. The one that you sent word down to not allow in the building anymore. He's here."

My gut clenched. "Then send him away."

"I did. I tried. But he won't go," Stu replied, exasperated. He clearly wasn't used to an omega that wouldn't listen. "I can call the police, but I remembered you saying you didn't like it when—"

"No, no, don't call the authorities." Many of them were upstanding alphas and betas looking to keep Wolf's Peak safe, but some of them were not. And when a person had that much power over another, it wasn't worth the risk. "I'll…deal with him." I was surprised I could keep my voice level as I spoke. If I had my way, I'd never have to see Wynn again.

No, that was a lie. If I had my way, Wynn would've stayed in my bed until morning when I made us both pancakes with smiley faces, and then we would've spent the rest of that day in bed as well. But I wasn't going to get what I wanted, and if Wynn was here to try to explain his side of things, he wasn't going to get what he wanted either.

He likely didn't know that I worked with such sensitive information. I didn't keep much at my house, but I was still very private about what I shared. Wynn had been the first person I'd let into my home since the last time my parents had visited.

"Sir?" Stu said when I moved to follow him.

"Yes?"

"Do you want to maybe… put on a shirt? And you have some meat." He pointed to my chin. "Just there."

I wiped my face. Stu had a point. "Tell him to wait in the lobby and that I am coming down."

Stu nodded.

"But also tell him I am very busy and don't have a lot of time." I felt petty the moment I'd spoken, but I tried to ignore it. I hurried to my bathroom, washing my face and brushing my teeth before deciding a shower was probably in order after two days of sloven wolf living. I picked a suit I usually wore to company picnics or outdoor events. It was casual but still dressed up enough that he would see just what he was missing. At the last second, I pulled a comb through my hair and gave myself a little spritz of cologne.

I told myself this little deception was fine. Wynn would have likely done the same thing. I wondered if he would be wearing the same demure style of outfit from before, or if he would have dressed more provocatively to grab my attention. Well, it wouldn't work. I was immune to his charms and would listen to whatever he had to say long enough to reply with a resounding F-off.

But, when I stepped out of the elevator, adjusting my bow tie so that it was straight, I spotted Wynn on the other side of the lobby, looking out the window to the traffic beyond. It had been another gloomy day, but the rain had hung off until just this moment. During our park outing, I'd worried that Wynn would think I had somehow controlled the weather, making it rain. Now I wondered if it was really him with that sort of power.

His cotton t-shirt was sky blue and wrinkly in the back. He wore casual jeans and had his hands stuffed in his pockets. I couldn't see his face, but I could see the upper edge of the mark I'd given him. That had been inappropriate. Mating marks were for mates, alphas and omegas who had agreed to live the rest of their lives together.

I smiled, pleased that he'd gone back to whoever it was he answered to with my mark on him. *That's an asshole thing to be happy for.* Yeah, well, no wolf was perfect.

Except that got me thinking about the type of person

he answered to. An alpha, for sure. And a powerful one, since no less would be able to control a man like Wynn. Was he some big shot in the entertainment industry? The type of alpha that had omegas dripping from every side of him? Wynn deserved better than that.

We both did.

"What is it?" I said to his back when I was four feet away.

He turned, giving me the first look at his face. His cheeks were white, and his golden eyes were dull. Not rimmed red as they might be if he wanted me to believe he'd been crying. But just dead, like the spirit that had been in him before was gone. It was a look he couldn't fake.

My eyes skidded over his mating mark to his arms. Just above his elbows on both sides were bruises. Not just one that he might've gotten from bumping into something, but as many as three on each side. Like fingers gripping him.

I reached for his wrist, keeping my touch firm but gentle enough that he could pull away *without* getting a mark. "What is this?" I asked him, unable to keep the growing anger out of my tone. "Who did this to you?"

Wynn did pull away, folding his arms across his chest. "I... the man I work for. He was—upset."

His pimp. Wynn had returned without me as a new client, and this was what had happened. "He did this to you? What is his name? Where does he live?"

I'd handle this like we handled this sort of thing in South Side. With fists and teeth. But first I'd make sure Wynn was nowhere near the violence.

"I can't tell you that," Wynn said, shaking his head. "The man I work for is..." He shuddered. "I don't want you anywhere near him."

"Wynn," I said his name softly, gently. "You can't go back to him. Not if he hurts you. I know it feels like you don't have choices, but you do. I know of programs you can go into. They can hide you from him until you are able to stand on your own feet."

"I *can* stand on my own feet," Wynn snapped, his spine as straight as a pole. "This didn't have anything to do with you, okay? It was something else and it's over now, so you don't have to worry."

I led us the corner of the lobby where there was a fireplace and a few armchairs. Stu watched our journey from behind the desk, no doubt wondering when I was going to get to the kicking out part of what I'd come down here to do. "But if he hurt you this time, he'll hurt you again." I sat up, taking deep breaths to calm myself before I asked my next question. "Is he *your* alpha? You didn't ask me to mark you—it was an instinct—but if that made things worse..."

Wynn covered the base of his neck with his palm, and I hated that the world couldn't see my mark on him even for this short amount of time. "It didn't make things any easier," he grumbled, but I was just glad he was telling me the truth.

And he was. I found I could tell between his truths and lies. The lies always made my neck itch, but so far I hadn't felt so much as a tickle. Not on the back of my neck, anyway. The rest of me was a mess of testosterone. I wanted to protect, to claim, but I'd kicked Wynn out of my house, was coming down here to kick him out of my building. I didn't have a right to do either.

"This is why they should teach omegas self-defense in grade school," I told him.

That got a small smile out of him.

"It isn't as difficult as you are probably thinking. A few well-timed moves, putting pressure in the right spots, and you can incapacitate an alpha at least long enough for you to run away." I reached forward for his hand and was glad when he let me hold it.

"Is that all it would take?" Wynn asked, still smiling.

I figured there was a joke I wasn't getting, but I didn't mind being teased a little if it meant Wynn coming out of this a little better able to protect himself. "Yes, that's all." I stood, pulling him up with me. "Come on. We're going."

"Where?" he asked shyly.

I swallowed my growl. I didn't want shy Wynn. I certainly didn't want dead-eyed Wynn. For the second time since knowing him, three if I counted the first, I knew what he was and made the choice not to care. I wanted the Wynn I'd been with the day before. The ostentatious, confident, authentic omega I'd begun to fall for. "To my gym. I'm teaching you how to defend yourself."

***

Wynn pulled up the gym shorts he'd borrowed from me. I told him I could buy him his own workout gear, but he'd insisted on it not being necessary. And honestly, if his shorts fell a little… I wouldn't mind.

Except you should mind because clearly he is involved with some other alpha, and you are on the fast track to future misery.

I knew that was the truth. I just didn't care. And maybe a tiny bit of me thought I could steal Wynn away from that life. Omegas that survived unmated didn't do so without learning a few tricks, finding safe harbors. This other alpha had likely been his safe harbor. *Well, thank you for keeping my omega safe, whoever you are, but your efforts are no longer necessary.*

I'd reserved one of the exercise rooms with a wall of mirrors so Wynn could watch his form and pads on the ground in case he fell. After I shut the door, blocking all the curious eyes, Wynn seemed to relax a little more. He stood in front of me, his shoulders lopsided as he kept a tight hand on the waistband of his shorts on one side. "You'll need both hands," I murmured, moving slowly to give him a chance to step away if he wanted to. He didn't. Not when I lifted the hem of my shirt he borrowed—that dangled on his smaller frame—and not when I folded open the waistband to reveal the drawstring.

He stood silently, his round, golden eyes on my face as I grabbed the strings and pulled them as tight as they would go, tying them in a bow to keep the string in place. "Usually, alphas try to take my pants off," Wynn joked.

I smiled, but inside, my wolf barked angrily. He didn't want anyone else pulling off this omega's pants.

My pants—I reminded myself.

But I wasn't so deluded as to believe that since he wore my pants, he was mine...

Right?

"Since you can't avoid dangerous alphas altogether, we're going to concentrate on explosive movements, maximum amounts of violence in the shortest time possible so that you can..." I waited for Wynn to fill in the blank.

"Find a weapon?" Wynn asked with a small smile.

"Close, so you can run. Running is your goal. Well, first your goal is to get to the side of your opponent that has no weapons. Stand in front of me here. What are my weapons?"

Wynn did as I asked, but with his lips turned up in the corner. I understood. Teaching an omega self-defense would be the same as teaching a cat ballet in some people's eyes. But if more omegas knew even simple maneuvers, then the quality of their lives would improve.

"Your fists," Wynn answered. I thought he was finished and opened my mouth to list the others, but he continued. "Your knees, elbows, feet and teeth."

I blinked at *teeth*. It wasn't one I normally thought of. "Yes, good, that's good. So your objective is to get on the side of my body where I can't use those weapons as effectively. Let's try this at first. Simply dodge around me—you're fast so we'll use that to our advantage. When you get to my dead side, I want you to kick in the general direction of my knee. The great thing about knees is that they are vulnerable from just about every direction. You kick, incapacitate your attacker, and then run. For now, just a practice kick, fifty percent speed, twenty percent power. Got it?" I was throwing a lot at him and was prepared to repeat myself, but he just nodded.

We stood off, me taking the place of the attacker while

he stood in the part of the victim. Only, as I got into position, I felt that itch at the back of my neck. Wynn wasn't saying anything so he couldn't be lying, but my intuition still told me something was off.

"Ready?" I asked, watching the way he sunk low in a stance I hadn't taught him yet. Maybe it was instinct? "Go!"

Wynn moved so quickly I couldn't track him. I felt a tap at my knee, and then all of a sudden, he was on the other side of the training room.

"How was that?" Wynn asked, trotting back.

"Really good," I replied, because it was. The itch at my neck increased. "Let's move on."

I taught him how to make a C-clamp and how to grip me at my weakest points, just above my elbow and at my neck. We practiced him kneeing me in the groin in this way, which he did flawlessly as well. In fact, everything I taught him, he picked up quickly. He really seemed to be paying attention and trying his hardest, so why couldn't I get rid of the feeling that he wasn't being honest?

About an hour later, his movements became more sluggish.

"I know you're tired, but you gotta keep your jabs fast, Wynn. Explode with aggression. You need to hit first and ask questions never because you'll be too far down the street for anyone to ask you shit. I know that's hard to wrap your head around. You've been taught the opposite all your life, but this is important, Matty." The moment the name came out of my mouth, I wanted to suck it back in.

Wynn froze in the middle of his movement, his hand raised, ready to grip the flesh of my arm. "Who is Matty? The boy in the picture?"

I'd forgotten that Wynn had seen those old photos. I could hardly look at them. "He was my brother. An omega. He died." I waited for the clawing rage, the overwhelming sadness, every powerful emotion that always reared up in me whenever I thought of my brother and what had happened to him. How I hadn't kept him safe. While the sadness and anger were there, neither was as powerful as normal. Maybe because I was doing what I'd promised at his funeral.

Wynn set his hand on my forearm. "Do you want to talk about it? About him?"

The itch disappeared in the face of his authentic concern. My usual answer to that question was no. I hadn't wanted to talk about it with my friends, not with the counselors my parents made me go to afterward, and not to anyone else who had asked about him in the years that followed. I was more concerned with what to do next. Who the fuck cared how I felt when my brother wasn't going to feel anything again?

I was a grown man now, though. Past my awkward baby alpha stage. Past my angry at the world stage. Older than this omega by at least ten years.

But it wasn't my position as an older alpha that made me want to share. It was the omega asking.

"We were born exactly a year apart. During the three months my omega dad was pregnant, they both let me know I'd be getting a baby brother who would need me. For the rest of our lives, my dads told me I needed to watch after Matty, to care for him. That the world wasn't kind to his types, not the way they were to me."

"Your parents were progressive," Wynn replied, sliding the hand from my forearm to my hand and tugging me down to sit on the mat.

"They are part of why I am who I am. And I listened to their warnings. Matty and I were inseparable. Where I went, he followed. But as we grew up, Matty became resentful of my protection. Not of me, but of living in a world where my protection was necessary at all. He started branching out, spreading his wings, going on dates." I stopped, overcome by the memory. When I spoke again, it felt like my words came from a distance, whispered from the past to our ears in the present. "He'd been so excited to be asked out on a date by the most sought after alpha who lived on our block. Victor.

"I'd grown up with Victor. His brother Veryl sometimes reminded me of Matty, though he was an alpha and just wanted to follow his brother around because he idolized him. I'd gone to school with Victor. Had no reason not to trust him. When Matty had left for his date, he'd looked so handsome, but mostly because he'd been so excited. It was the last time I ever saw him alive."

Wynn's hand clenched over mine. "What happened to Victor?"

The question came out tightly, angrily, like my answer was going to govern what Wynn did next. It also told me that Wynn understood this world on a level that Matty never had. He'd assumed familiar meant safe. So had I. "He's in prison." A small mercy. Many alphas never saw justice for their crimes. But Matty had grown up by my side. "Matty had been loved by many. All my friends had watched him as if he was their own little brother. When the police came around, barely doing their jobs, they found a community more than willing to put Victor and Matty together at the time of his murder. And Victor had left enough evidence of his own that we were able to secure a conviction. Barely."

"That's good. Alphas like that never stop." Wynn squeezed my hand. "Which means you can't blame yourself. He was a predator, waiting patiently for his moment to strike. If it didn't happen then, it would've happened another time."

Plenty of people had told me not to blame myself, none in the way Wynn did. As if he had more than his fair share of experience with alphas who attacked.

What was I thinking? Of course he did. I forgot what he was at every turn.

That thought made me want to protect him more, to pin him to my side as I'd done Matty. Until I hadn't.

"Let's go," I said, rising smoothly while pulling him

with me.

"Where to?" Wynn asked, though he walked easily beside me.

***

Two hours later, we were in the elevator of my building. Stu beamed at us when we returned. I was beginning to doubt the sincerity of his exasperation from earlier. I couldn't be upset with him if Wynn had managed to bring him under his thrall as well. It was an easy place to fall.

As the elevator rose, Wynn stared at the small cylinder on its side in the palm of his hand. We'd gone to the security and defense outlet, and while I'd wanted to buy the place out of their defense items, he'd allowed me to buy him only one item. I'd chosen pepper spray since it didn't require him to be near his attacker.

Wynn had accepted the gift silently and had stayed that way. At the store, I worried I was frightening him. During the cab back, I thought maybe I'd overstepped my boundaries. But now I wasn't sure how to decipher his expression. Amused sadness was as close a descriptor as I could come up with.

"We can practice with it, if you aren't sure you can use it when the time comes," I said, my voice sounding too loud in the elevator. When the double doors opened and we walked inside, Wynn set the pepper spray and the bag it had come in down on the counter. He turned toward me, and I waited for the fight that I was sure was about to come.

His body became a blur as he launched toward me, leaping and reaching his arms around my neck as he brought his legs up to wrap around my waist. I caught him, since the alternative was letting him fall.

His lips were on mine. A frenzy of desperate kisses followed, each needier than the one that came before. I growled low, kissing him back, but he'd initiated this, and clearly, he wanted to be the one to lead. I massaged the supple globes of his ass the whole time, stumbling around my apartment like a blind fish waiting to bump into a worm. I managed to hit my sofa and brought us both down. He straddled my lap, but his pants were too tight for me to feel his cock. If it was anything like mine, it was rock hard and longing to be released.

Everything with Wynn felt like foreplay. Teaching him earlier in the gym, walking from the gym to the defense store, the cab ride back—all of it had fueled this lusty fire between us. And now, we'd become an inferno.

Except, until this moment, I thought I'd been the only one affected. It was impossible to still think that now as Wynn humped against me, trying to create a friction that his clothing wouldn't allow.

Had I woken up that morning cursing his name? That felt like it had happened a million years ago. All it took for me to forgive Wynn was to be near him.

"Stay the night, Wynn," I murmured against his mouth.

He buried his face into my neck, licking and sucking as he reached under my shirt, grazing his nails over my abs, up my chest, where he used the jagged end of one of his fingernails to circle a nipple like a shark. He squeezed the puckered peak, making me gasp. While both the noise I'd made and the sensation of having my nipple pinched were new, I found I enjoyed both. I liked that my omega could make me moan as well as I could him.

But he still hadn't responded to my request.

"Wynn, stay with me."

He ripped his mouth free and stared down at me. His lips were swollen and even more red than usual. His eyes shone with desire, and something else that looked a lot like fear. Of me?

"Wynn—"

"I can't," he wailed, his voice tortured.

I forced my hands to remain relaxed. "Why? Because of that alpha? The one who gave you this?" I pulled his arm straight so we could both stare at the marks I hated. "Is he your mate, Wynn?"

"No!" Wynn replied before I could even finish my question. "But. He is part of the reason. Yes. I'm supposed to…" He took a deep breath, and I was glad for it because he looked like he might pass out. "I'm supposed to do something I don't want to do."

I couldn't stop my deep growl. It rumbled through us both. "He's forcing you?"

Wynn turned his head toward the wall of windows. "Please, I don't want to spend this time talking about him."

To keep us both calm, I began trailing my fingers down his spine, from neck to tailbone. I dragged my hands down, lifted them and brought them back down again. He slumped against me, both of us quiet for several minutes. When he let out a contented sigh, I craned my head back to see into his face. "Maybe I could talk to him?"

Immediately, Wynn stiffened.

I hated how quickly he could go from content to on edge. It was as if he'd lived a life where danger lurked around every corner, more than the average omega experienced. I wanted to protect him, was here practically begging for him to let me, and he wouldn't even entertain the thought. How was I supposed to convince him to let me into the fortress of his mind when he wouldn't even let me shove my foot in the door?

"Can't we go back to kissing?" he asked quietly. He often seemed so wise; it was easy for me to forget that he was younger. Only around four years older than Matty had been when he'd been murdered.

"Yes, we can," I said, cupping his face and kissing him softly. Despite my attempts to keep it sweet, it wasn't long before our kisses warmed back up. I thrust my tongue forward, meeting his and twining around it as I shoved my hand down the back of his pants, delving between his cheeks where I tickled his ass.

"Magnus," he wailed. Again, the noise was tortured.

Suddenly, I knew exactly what my omega needed. His

scent had thickened, coating my tongue and throat, dripping down into my body and filling me with the essence of his need. He was going into heat.

This light, it wasn't a full-blown heat, but in a day, he'd be begging for an alpha's knot. My chest rumbled. Was this his normal cycle? A spontaneous heat? "Wynn—" I croaked.

"Please, Magnus. No more talking. I know I need you. Can't we focus on that?"

Yes. We could. I could satisfy my omega without putting him in danger. I pulled off his shirt in a single motion and dropped it to the ground, my hands going for the buttons at his pants. While I worked them free, I turned on the sofa so that I could recline lengthwise. Wynn rotated with me, and in this new position I was able to slip his pants down to his hips before the angle made it impossible.

"Just tear them off me," he cried out.

I didn't need to be told twice. I shifted enough to allow my nails to grow and sharpen. His pants fell away, still stuck under him in the places where our bodies touched, but his front was clear of the fabric that had separated us. His dick stretched his underwear in the front. At the tip of the tent was a wet spot from where he'd leaked precum. I needed to taste him.

Gripping him at the waist, I brought his body forward so that he didn't straddle my lap, but my face. I reached under the waistband of his underwear and pulled him free. There wasn't time for teasing or drawing it out. I needed him in my mouth. Now.

I stretched my neck forward and let his solid length slip inside my mouth. Wynn moaned, one hand gripping the back of the sofa while the other held onto my head. I hummed around his length, easily fitting the whole thing into my mouth. The tip bumped against my tonsils, and he groaned. My omega liked that.

I sucked hard as I pulled back, taking deep, long,

deliberate strokes with my mouth, all the while my tongue licked over his velvety hardness.

The scent of his arousal strengthened as a shot of precum exploded on my tongue. He was so sweet. Like candy. Like sunshine and fields of flowers. Like a happy life of picnics and smiles.

He tasted like he was mine.

He whimpered, and I realized he was speaking.

"I need you too," he was saying, wiggling to reach my pants. I understood in the next second and lifted his petite frame, giving him the leverage necessary to undo my pants, to push them down enough so that my dick could spring free.

I spun him in the next moment on both his horizontal and vertical axis so that he landed face down—more importantly, dick down—and back inside my mouth.

He sucked me inside the warm depths of his mouth with the same amount of vigor, bringing the hand not holding himself up down to cup and fondle my balls. I was larger, and he had more trouble swallowing my length. His body convulsed as he gagged, the motion making his muscles constrict over the head of my dick.

I thought to tell him that he didn't have to do that, if it was too much. I didn't want him to hurt himself. But he was as eager as he was talented, and I feared if I stopped for even a moment, I'd orgasm way before him.

And that was an embarrassment I'd rather avoid—at least while I was still trying to convince him of my ability to protect him as an alpha.

I increased the speed, taking my cue from the tenor of his hums. I brought him deep, letting him linger there for a moment before shaking my head, massaging his cock in different ways. Wynn wailed, pausing his efforts for just long enough to let the cry escape his mouth, vibrating over my dick.

He went still, tensing every muscle in his body while he lingered on the edge of orgasm. With my mouth on his dick, I spread his ass apart, massaging his pucker with sure strokes.

My omega fell apart, suddenly boneless as he cried out and spilled into my mouth. The small taste I'd gotten earlier was nothing compared to this outpouring of sweet nectar.

And even while he came, he continued to suck my length, adding his hands to the mix, wrapping both around my length and pumping me in time with his mouth. "Fuck, Wynn!" I roared toward the heaven as I thrust my hips up, in and out of his mouth as he took my seed.

I lifted him off me and turned him back around so that our heads were on the same side. His mouth glistened both with saliva and remnants of my cum. I growled, bringing our lips together. If I hadn't, I would have laid my claim right then and there, explaining in clear and certain terms that he was mine, that he was staying here, that he would never have to leave.

And while that was the only thing I wanted to tell him, I kissed him instead because I knew this omega couldn't be ordered around. He needed to be wooed, won.

And I intended to do just that.

CHAPTER EIGHT
Wynn

Magnus was in the shower, the door open allowing me to hear the water that rushed over his body. I could imagine the way the water would sluice down, disappearing in the thick hairs at the base of his dick before pouring over his thighs and continuing down his legs.

I knew he'd left the door open in the hopes that I'd join him in the shower, but I needed to think without his alpha pheromones clouding my judgment.

We hadn't fucked, a meaningless distinction to anyone but myself. But even though we hadn't crossed that boundary again, this day had changed everything.

I squeezed my hand over the container of pepper spray. Often, the caustic spray did as much damage to the victim as the attacker, since it sprayed without a lot of accuracy into the air. I knew what it felt like to get a full pepper spray blast to the face. It had been a part of our training in the OAC. We'd lined up as a team as the instructor emptied a large canister—meant for public riots—over and around our heads.

The burning wasn't anywhere near as bad as the coughing the spray induced. Mixing that with the buckets of mucous that a body produced when confronted with the stuff, and it was easy to feel like you were drowning while standing on dry land.

But Magnus hadn't known that. Just like he hadn't known I could have incapacitated him in a thousand different ways before I'd need to resort to running. He cared. He worried. He wanted me to be safe.

He wasn't a monster.

I sighed, letting that realization settle in my head like new bricks in a wall.

He wasn't a monster, and Taft was wrong. Except I didn't have any idea how to go about convincing him of that. I'd brought up my concerns, my instinct, and he'd ignored it. At the time, I'd thought that meant he knew something I didn't. Now I wasn't so sure.

But I *was* sure that if I didn't show up at the OAC headquarters before too long, they would track my location using my phone and would bring me back, assigning a new omega assassin to Magnus in the process.

Magnus couldn't die. He wasn't like the men I'd killed before now. He was good and caring and honest.

Did I continue looking for the information the clients wanted? The omega tracking technology? If I had that, maybe I could use it as a bargaining chip to spare Magnus's life.

The OAC was the only life I knew. What would they do if I rebelled now?

And did the unknown consequence matter when the alternative was a world without Magnus?

I wished I could contact my team. Even if they didn't have any more answers than I did, River would have a few kind words of comfort, Van would have something clever to add that I hadn't thought of, and Zed was at least good for a few distracting moments in the practice ring.

Even bickering with Nolan would have been a welcomed respite to the uncertainty I felt now.

The water turned off, and my heart jumped into my throat. My time was up, but I wasn't any closer to knowing what I should do.

I pulled my phone from my pants that were still balled up on the floor.

"Wynn?" Magnus asked, coming up behind me.

His voice, his closeness, triggered a response in me, answering my questions. I peeled the back casing off my phone, pried the battery free, and then used my fingernail to slide out the inner identity module from the slot.

"Babe, what are you doing?"

I dropped the pieces and rose quickly, grabbing Magnus's toned shoulders. He smelled of his soap, clean but woodsy. "Let's get out of here."

"Get out of where? The bedroom?"

I knew I sounded crazy, but that was fine because I felt that way as well. "No, downtown, this place, this world. Let's go somewhere. Disappear. It can be just us, and we won't have to worry about anything, anyone. It will be just us." I clung to him, and thankfully he let me.

His warm hands wrapped around my middle. "How am I supposed to deny you anything when you're completely naked?"

I smiled as the weight of my worry lifted off my shoulders. We could run. I didn't have to choose.

"Should I be concerned? If this about you worrying about me coming face to face with that alpha—"

It was, and it wasn't. I didn't enjoy the idea of Taft and Magnus going head to head. The way Taft had reacted to Magnus thus far was reason enough to believe them being in the same room together would be a bad thing. But that concern was secondary to what I was, what I'd been sent to do. If I told him, what would that change? How could he ever forgive my past?

I wished I'd been a hooker all along. At least that was something Magnus had no problem looking past.

I kissed him instead of answering. While his lips moved against mine and he held me to him, I knew there would be questions later. That was fine, as long as it was later. "I just want to go, get out of the city."

He kissed me and then pulled his head back to look into my eyes. "Wynn, we haven't been together very long, but I would fight for you. You know that, right? If there is something, *someone* you are running from, just tell me. I'll fix it. I may not be a typical alpha, but I'm still an alpha. I can protect you."

I smiled. It didn't matter if he was correct or not. It mattered that he'd offered. Magnus wanted to protect me.

What a strange idea.

I wondered if that was the real reason why I didn't want to tell him who I was, why I'd thrust myself into his life. If he knew what I was capable of, would he still feel the need to protect me? "I just want to get out of here and go where I can be someone different."

"I know just the place."

***

I'd watched the landscape outside my window change from tightly packed blocks full of mega skyscrapers to streets stuffed with houses, rows and rows of them crammed with people all living on top of each other. Magnus seemed pensive during the drive so he didn't talk much, and I was so worried he'd change his mind that I stayed silent as well.

I didn't ask many questions about where we were going. His file had been sparse when it came to his life before he'd started his business, so I wasn't worried about being found wherever we went. And while I still had the pieces of my phone in my hastily packed bag—that was full of only things Magnus had lent me—as long as it remained unassembled, I would be safe from the OAC tracker pinging our location.

With each mile that we drove out of the city, I felt lighter. I wasn't the assassin sent to kill the man sitting next to me. I was an omega lucky enough to find an alpha who wanted to take care of me.

Magnus's phone began to ring, and he used a button on

the steering wheel to answer, setting the call on speaker mode.

"Mag, please tell me you're still coming home!" a deep voice said immediately as if they were already in the middle of a conversation.

"Yes, Dad, I'm coming now. Only twenty minutes out of the exit. And I'm bringing...someone." He looked over at me as if unsure of what to call me.

I held my hand out for him to grab, and he did, balancing our hands on the gear shift.

"Claude! Claude! He said he's bringing someone," Magnus's dad said, speaking away from the phone.

"Dad! Hold on, you don't have to scream and tell the neighborhood. It's still really new, what I have with my omega, but yeah, he's special to me, and you'll both meet him when I get there—"

"He's in the car right now? He's hearing this?" The voice rose in pitch.

"Yeah," Magnus replied, drawing the word out.

"I—well, warn a guy next time!" his dad replied. "I've got your room all set up, but I can make the bed in the guest room just as easily for—"

"Dad, you don't need to go out of your way—"

"It isn't going out of my way to make a guest feel welcomed."

"I'm a guest now? I know it's been a while since I've been hom—"

"Not you! Your friend. Oh my, it will be nice to have another omega in the house. Your father is lovely, but sometimes he simply can't understand. Does your omega cook? We can bake something. Or maybe we can—"

"Dad, he's still here, listening to every word," Magnus said with a laugh. "How about I just get there and then we can make plans. It will probably be easier for us to stay in a hotel anyway."

"A hotel?" I could tell Magnus's dad didn't like the sound of that. "We'll just talk about it when you get here, honey. Drive safe." He must not have hung up very quickly because we could still hear him talking, though he was clearly not speaking into the phone. "Can you believe it, Claude? He's coming home!"

Magnus hit the button to end the call before giving me a sheepish expression. "When I left South Side, I told them I'd be back often to visit. It's only a few hours outside of downtown, but that didn't end up happening. I should probably thank you for making me go back."

He was taking me to meet his parents.

Once, I'd been sent on a mission with some truly horrendous intel. The clients had been grieving, so eager to get the alpha responsible for taking their omega son away that they hadn't bothered verifying anything they'd been told, including the whereabouts of the alpha in question or who else lived on the premises. A lot of people did, it turned out. All armed. Even then, hunched behind a wheelbarrow in that alpha's yard while taking on heavy fire, I hadn't been as nervous as I was at this exact moment.

Magnus squeezed my hand. "Are you okay with this? I'm only now thinking about how maybe, going to my hometown to meet my parents possibly wasn't what you'd imagined."

"I've never done this before." My voice sounded young. "My parents died when I was a child. They weren't really great parents before that, either."

He brought my hand up, kissing my knuckles. "They'll love you," he said, and though that was the type of thing an alpha would tell an omega months after knowing them and not days, I still believed him. "And if they don't like you, they'll be too polite to admit it anyway."

He laughed, and I yanked my hand free, smacking him between the ribs.

"Ouch!" He rubbed at the spot. "Remind me never to be on your bad side."

A giggle escaped my mouth, followed quickly by a

second. When the third made it hard to breathe I decided I was experiencing some sort of delayed anxiety attack.

I was off-grid, AWOL. If Taft hadn't noticed already, it would take only a few more hours before he sounded the alarm on my disappearance.

What would he do when he couldn't find me? What would my team do?

"You crawled back inside that head."

I looked over at Magnus, finding him already looking at me. "You need to watch the road," I murmured, squirming as my body warmed in response to his stare.

While my impulsive action was catching up to me, I couldn't regret who I'd chosen to join me.

That's the line I kept repeating the rest of the drive south whenever panic would try to settle in. By the time Magnus turned down a street lined with a row of red brick houses, I was still relatively calm. Despite the evening hour, there were a few people out on the sidewalk, more gathered in casual groups on the steps of some of the houses. Everyone peered through the windshield, some smiling with recognition when they spotted Magnus.

No one smiled at me.

"It's like I never left. Oh shit, that's Clipper and Pat, I thought they'd gone off to college." Magnus pulled the car over and pressed the button to roll down his window. "Can you tell me how to get to your dad's house? I'm late for a date." Magnus asked, a wide smile on his face.

The two men, both alphas, were silent for the space of a second before they recognized Magnus and leapt forward, all smiles and boisterous laughs. "Look who finally fell out of their golden tower! What are you doing here slumming it?"

"Sometimes, you just need to get away," Magnus replied easily. "I don't think this should be a problem, but just in case, no one saw us, okay?"

The taller of the two grabbed his chest, and play stumbled back as if he was having a heart attack. "You wound us. I'll forgive this time since you've been gone so long, but South Siders don't snitch. Especially not to outsiders. Now, speaking of outsiders..." He poked his head through the window, looking at me and waggling his eyebrows. "Hey there."

"Hello," I replied with a smile.

Magnus leaned forward, squeezing his friend out from in front of him. "He's taken, and he isn't here either, got it?" While his words were friendly, there was a layer of serious intent.

The friend leaned back, raising his hands in surrender. "Got it, bro, understood."

Magnus said his goodbyes, promising to meet up with them sometime before we left. "I spent so many hours standing around just like that."

"What did you all do all that time?"

"What did we do?" Magnus asked. "Babe, we solved the world's problems. We just never left the stoop long enough to put our plans in action."

"Until you did."

"That's a nice way of putting it. Though it isn't wrong. Many of the security devices I invented with MattyCorp came from ideas that started right here. The safety chip that we're about to launch included."

I sat a little straighter. Magnus hadn't mentioned his newest project until now. "The chip? What does it do?"

Magnus watched me for a long second, and I worried that I'd overstepped. He was on to me. "This is pretty dangerous information. Think you can handle it?"

"Don't tell me anything you'll regret." Part of me wanted to tell him to tell me nothing at all.

"You are always so surprising in the best ways. I'll admit, the chip is over ten years in the making and will fulfill part of a promise I made to my brother while we buried him. It wasn't difficult installing a GPS tracking unit, but for the chip to also activate closed-circuit recording in the area was a process of trial and error. We couldn't have the chips bind up the cameras for long periods of time, but simply knowing where an omega is and recording audio wasn't enough. Not with how difficult it is to get a conviction." He stopped talking, pulling to the side of the road in front of one of a row of brick houses. "We're here."

Now that he'd started talking, I wished he would explain the rest of the chip. Some of the information lined up with what I'd been told—a device that would constantly monitor the location of any omega—but the intent behind the device was completely different than the intent I'd been told. Could it be that Taft was confused as well?

Or was he knowingly setting me up to kill an alpha that didn't deserve it?

I couldn't begin to worry about that. It threatened to open a flood of what-ifs. And my earlier squirming that I'd thought had been a reaction from Magnus looking at me was beginning to feel more like something else. Something that I forgot to pack for.

Fuck, fuck, fuck. The way I felt now, I probably still had a few hours, maybe half a day before my heat kicked in, but it was surely on the horizon.

Magnus had gotten out and walked around to my side, opening the door and reaching a hand to help me to the pavement. That light contact sent a zing up my arm.

I sucked in a smoggy breath and let it out slowly. The last thing I needed to do was become a horny mess in front of Magnus's parents.

He grabbed my hand as we walked to the stoop, the front door flying open before we'd climbed the second step.

"My son! My alpha son is home!" A tall, thin man burst out of the doorway. He came at us in a sprint, but at the last second, it looked like his toe caught on the edge of the welcome mat, and he started to go down. I could see this was about to get real ugly real quick if Magnus's omega dad slammed into the concrete steps. I lurched forward, but then his omega dad's body froze while actively in the position of falling. I peeked around him, spotting an older, muscled man holding a large handful of the omega's clothing, keeping him from falling completely forward.

With a grunt, he pulled the omega back, sliding him under his arm. "Welcome home, son," he said, his voice deep and rumbly like Magnus's.

"Thank you," the omega said to him sheepishly before turning back to us. "I am just so excited. Everything is how you left it. Exactly. And we have food! I mean, dinner. We have dinner. I made it." When he stopped speaking, it was as if everything he had said hit his ears, and he winced.

"I like dinner." I wasn't sure why I'd said as much, except that Magnus's omega dad seemed so eager and excited, and I didn't want him to be embarrassed on my account.

Magnus squeezed my hand, and then we were walking forward, up the stairs. We stopped just in front of them, but I'd evaluated every movement the four of us had made. I felt focused, like how I got right before I eliminated a target. Except I certainly didn't want to eliminate anyone here. I just didn't want to miss anything.

"Dads, this is Wynn. Wynn, this is Mr. and Mr. Gray."

"Nonsense. Call me Alex and my mate Claude." Alex burst out from under his alpha's arm and gave his son a hug, made awkward only because Magnus didn't let go of my hand during. When they were done, Alex angled his body toward me but hesitated. Had something in my body language conveyed that I didn't want to be touched? Or was it something else he sensed? Whatever it was, he resolved it because his arms wrapped around me. He was surprisingly strong for his size and demeanor, and he smelled like he'd spent the day in the kitchen working with spices. "It is so nice to meet you, Wynn," Alex whispered. "You don't know how long I've hoped for this exact moment."

That his alpha son would bring home the omega hired to kill him? I doubted he'd spent his nights hoping for that. *That's not who you are right now.* "Thank you for welcoming me into your home," I said.

"Something my mate has yet to do," Claude said with a smile. "Please, step off the stoop and come inside. Magnus indicated you have made other sleeping arrangements for tonight, but you must allow us to at least feed you."

I stepped into the narrow but tall home. The entryway was like a time capsule into Magnus's past. There were shots of him hanging on the stoop with his pals, of him and Matty in various locations, some of the four of them. In all of them they were smiling, beaming at the camera like they didn't have a worry in the world.

I spun in a complete circle looking at all the pictures hung on the wall. There had been times with my team, generally after a particularly hard training or mission, where we'd wondered together if perfect families existed. I had to commit every detail to memory because I'd found one.

Except, as we walked down the hallway, I noticed the ages in the pictures got to a certain point and then stopped. There was Magnus as a young adult and then nothing. I felt white-hot rage toward the alpha who had stopped this family from continuing to take beaming, happy photos. He was lucky he was in prison.

"Wynn?" Magnus asked softly, staring at my face.

I must've let some of my anger show—another in a long line of rookie mistakes that I couldn't stop making in front of Magnus. He made me forget my training. More than that, he let me forget who I was, if only for short bursts until something like this reminded me. "Sorry, I was just thinking."

"Don't worry. We'll make this quick."

I grabbed his hand to stop him from heading to the other room and following his parents. "We don't have to—make this quick, I mean." I couldn't tell him that this was the first happy family I'd ever experienced, and even though it all felt tinged with sadness, I just wanted to sit here and soak it up.

In the next room, Alex had a tray of crackers, cheese, and meats as well as a wine. He poured me a glass, but I thought about how I'd felt earlier and worried some of my behavior at Magnus's penthouse was due to my coming heat. I waved the wine away. Alcohol would only bring the symptoms on faster and stronger. "It's probably for the best that I don't."

At that, Alex gasped, and Claude's smile stretched wider. I looked to Magnus, who had lost some of the color in his face. "I can have a sip..." I started to say, but Alex waved his hands rapidly in front of his body.

"No, don't do anything you don't want to. I just—I thought that you were saying that you were..."

I blinked, at a complete and total loss as to what they—

"Pregnant," Claude finished.

I choked on the cracker I'd been nibbling on. As chunks went down the wrong way and I tried to violently hack it up, I imagined myself swollen with a child. Carrying a life inside of me for three months. It wasn't so odd a thought. That was what omegas did, why they needed to be cared for and kept safe—at least that was the line alpha politicians always spun when trying to take away more omega rights. But the idea of me becoming pregnant—it had honestly never once crossed my mind. It wasn't like I could still work with the OAC with a big belly. And after. I knew I risked my life every time I went on a mission. It was an acceptable sacrifice, but with a child at home, how would that change?

And yet my skin warmed and tingled as if begging for my alpha's touch.

I needed to rein this in before it got out of control. "Excuse me, may I use the restroom?"

"Are you okay?" Magnus asked, getting to his feet, but

Alex beat him to it.

"You stay here. I'll show him." At that, he grabbed my elbow gently and led me out.

My skin itched under his palm. It wasn't the touch my wolf wanted, but I didn't pull out of his grasp. "I'm sorry if I gave you a fright back there. I can see that having children is not on your radar at the moment." Alex didn't sound disappointed. "I worried when my son became successful that his dedication to his job would make him blind to a pretty, young, omega face who just wanted his money. But if you wanted that, you'd be in a hurry to get pregnant."

While the idea of securing protection and a stable life by getting knocked up wasn't unheard of, it was not something I ever planned on doing to anyone ever. "That's not the type of person I am," I said, trying and failing to keep all the ice out of my tone.

"No, it isn't, is it?" Alex replied with a soft smile. "I know that Magnus makes being an honorable man look easy, but it doesn't come without effort. He fights his more brutish alpha urges, just as his father must, so that they can be good men. I am protective of him retaining that humanity. Sometimes I think I am more protective of that than either of them are of me."

Which was only proof of how much it mattered to Alex.

"I'm not trying to hurt him." In fact, I was doing the opposite.

"I believe you," Alex replied, gesturing to a door to our right. "The bathroom. When you're finished, we're down this hallway." He pointed. "Or you can just wander around. We have no secrets here."

Must be nice.

"I'll be right out. Unless you were lying about the dinner?"

Alex laughed softly, like the tinkle of a small bell. "I never lie," he said, giving me a half hug. "Thank you for bringing back my son. I think, until he had you, home was just too sad of a place for him to want to go."

I nodded, unsure of what to do. Hug him back? Say "you're welcome?" I could disarm a man twice my size with a plastic straw but had no idea how to respond to a hug from a parent. Alex turned around, eager to get back to visiting.

In the bathroom, I splashed water over my face and breathed deeply. I just had to keep my thoughts away from anything sexual, avoid alcohol, and I would be fine. For now. I'd figure it out later.

I finished up and went back to the main room. I hadn't meant to start eavesdropping, but I was a naturally quiet walker, and old habits died hard.

"He's younger than you," Claude said, I assumed to Magnus.

"Dad was younger than you when you met," Magnus replied.

I heard rustling, possibly an embrace between Alex and Claude. I knew I should've walked the rest of the way into the room, but I was frozen now.

"He's nice. But skittish," Alex said. So the omega saw more than he let on. Should I have expected anything different from the parents of Magnus? "Do you know what happened to him? I know that you want to believe you can fix everything, but—"

"Look, I know he's younger than me. I know he's scared, but he's still here, isn't he? I saw his face when he found out where we were going. He was terrified. But he's still here, by my side. Even though he's scared, even though we just met. That means more to me than anything. In fact, it convinces me that there is nothing we can't work through."

"You're serious about this. About him?" Claude asked.

"Yes, one hundred percent."

"Then maybe we should invite him in from the hallway and continue to dinner?"

Busted.

I walked in then, my face red. But there was no anger waiting for me. Just smiles.

"Don't worry, son. I would've done the same thing," Claude said, getting to his feet.

Magnus slipped me under his arm, and I found it was a place I very much enjoyed being. His warm weight on my shoulder wasn't too heavy, but enough to let me know a solid, strong man stood by my side. One that would protect me, defend me from even his own parents. One that…

Just maybe…

I could see myself starting a family with. If that was something I was still capable of. *A family?*

Maybe there wasn't a way to consolidate my relationship with Magnus and the Omega Assassins Club. There never was one. *Maybe* I had to choose, one or the other.

Could I choose Magnus?

After dinner, we went back to the car. Magnus sat in the driver's seat for an extra moment before starting the car. His hands were tight around the steering wheel.

"What else do you do to help omegas?" I asked

At the exact same time, he asked, "Why didn't you mention your heat?"

We stared at each other. Then Magnus answered. "Everything I do at MattyCorp is to help make omega lives a little safer. But I've been thinking about other ways to help. Opening centers where omegas can stay protected, starting more defense classes like what we did the other day. It's just about getting people qualified to help me. Why? Do you want to help omegas, Wynn? What do you think? Should we save the world together?"

Tears pressed against the back of my eyes. "Yes," I whispered with a jerky nod. "I think we should. And I'm sorry about my heat. It snuck up on me. Was it obvious in there?"

"No, I don't think so. I sensed it earlier back at my house."

I couldn't tell him I'd forgotten my suppressors. Their existence on my person was grounds for immediate arrest. I wouldn't put him in that kind of danger. Besides, if I was going to live a life outside of the OAC, I was going to have to get used to suffering through them.

He started the car and pulled it out onto the road. There wasn't a lot of other traffic. Less than three minutes later, he pulled into another driveway. "I booked this hotel originally because I'd sensed it coming." He switched the dome light and turned toward me. "I booked us two rooms. Yours is connected to mine, but you don't have to… I mean, I'm not expecting you to—"

I leaned over and kissed him. Partly because my heat was starting to settle in, but mostly because this alpha constantly managed to surprise me with his consideration. Before Magnus, I hadn't believed alphas like him existed. I'd thought there were the bad ones and the ones that hadn't been bad yet. But now… I was questioning everything.

"Take me to bed, Magnus. I'll be gentle. I promise."

Magnus beamed. "Whatever you say, omega."

Magnus left me to check in, after politely asking that I stay in the car. Apparently, my scent was dragging out all of his protective urges. I agreed, waiting only a few minutes in the quiet parking lot. The hotel he'd drove us to wasn't even as large as the lobby floor of his apartment building. He came out, heading for the passenger door.

When he opened it, I stepped out, but he swooped me up in his arms. "Can you please forgive me this?" he asked, like carrying me was a bad thing.

I replied by nuzzling my cheek into his chest. His scent enveloped me, both the artificial smells from soaps and the masculine scent that was naturally his. The walk from the car to the room was brief, but by the time he slid the old fashioned key into the lock, I was hard. This heat was coming fast. I felt it in my limbs, making them heavier.

My breaths came more slowly, and I savored each one. I could taste Magnus on my tongue, like each breath was a lick over his skin. That thought brought a shiver of anticipation.

"Are you cold, my omega?" Magnus asked, squeezing me tighter.

Cold? I was burning up. But I didn't want to say anything that would relax Magnus's hold on me.

He carried me inside, closing the door immediately and locking it.

"Is this your room or mine?"

"Mine. Yours is through that door." He indicated a door that joined us. There were bars on this side and three locks.

"That's some high security."

"It's the, um, the *safe suite*. That was one of the first things I did after making my first chunk of real money. In this neighborhood, if an omega is going into heat without a safe space to lock themselves inside of, they can come to this hotel and ask for the safe suite. I have a contract with the owners that keeps it open and allows the omega in need to stay for up to a week, long enough for a heat to come and go. The doors are all double reinforced, bulletproof, and the ventilation system purifies the air before releasing it back outside so no one walking by is any the wiser."

I popped my head up, momentarily distracted. "I've never heard of anything like that before."

"My hope is for that to change. If not now, then with the next generation of omegas." He sounded determined. "I meant what I said. If you want to wait things out in there, the fridge is already stocked for you. As long as you don't mind me taking up post outside anyway."

"To do what?"

"Growl at the maintenance workers? Pace? Worry? I've got a full schedule, really."

I smiled, but my body was reaching the end of its capacity for polite conversation. "I don't want you to do any of that. And I don't want to writhe in horny pain for days either."

"Wynn, are you sure? I'm all in on this... whatever you want to call what we have, but you could get pregnant. You aren't worried?"

He didn't know that I'd already made the decisions that would change my life. "I'm all in too, Magnus. The life I had... I can't have that and you. So I don't want it. I want you. I just want you."

Magnus growled, and the noise felt like a gentle caress down my dick. He carried me to a large bed, setting me on top of the comforter as he returned to the door, checking the locks. When he was sure we were secure, he returned, laying beside me. "You're shaking," he said, placing his hand flat on my stomach.

My abs jumped and jolted beneath his touch. "I've never done this before." I was saying that a lot, but this time, Magnus just stared at me, his head tilted to the side in confusion. "Not sex!" I clarified once I realized what his expression was for. "I've had sex before, obviously. But... our boss, he didn't allow us to... I mean that he..." How did I tell him about the suppressors without telling him about the suppressors?

"He didn't want any of you getting pregnant?"

I nodded.

"So you've never been fulfilled during a heat?" I shook my head, and Magnus's gaze darkened with desire. "And you're choosing me?" he croaked as if the answer to that wasn't obvious. "I'll take care of you, Wynn."

I never worried he wouldn't.

"Wait here," he said before disappearing and making me frown. I heard the water running a few seconds later and guessed he was drawing a bath. Sure enough, a minute later, he returned with a white robe. "Change into this."

"What about you?" I asked, eying his fully clothed state.

102

"The bath is for you. I know that there is anxiety that comes with heats, particularly in someone as young as you."

I'd undressed and slipped the robe over my limbs. It felt scratchy against my sensitized skin, and I longed to feel only his skin instead. I'd been sporting an erection for a while, but feeling Magnus's gaze on my partially covered body made the rest of me ache.

I felt empty, which was ridiculous when I knew he had a cock that could more than fill me. "Magnus, you don't have to do all this extra stuff," I said, for once, not minding the whine.

"I do. You might not think so now, but later, when you look back, you'll be glad for the extra stuff."

That was yet another difference when it came to my life with Magnus. At the OAC, we didn't do a lot of talking about the future, about when we were old. The cruel truth was that many of us wouldn't grow old. We knew by observation and intelligence that the average life span of an assassin was shorter than most professions. But, with Magnus, it was as if I had my whole life ahead of me.

I let him carry me to the bathroom. He was careful not to touch my bare skin and let me lower myself into the water. I did so, slowly. I might later appreciate these kind gestures, but right now, I could tease him for it.

Magnus clenched his hands into fists and let out a groaning growl but remained where he was until I was completely beneath the layer of foamy bubbles.

"Where's the soap?" I asked.

Magnus reached behind his body, grabbing something off the counter before coming to the edge of the bath and dropping to his haunches. "You just lean back and relax. I'll handle everything." His voice had dipped low, giving me an idea of what *everything* was.

By this point, I would beg for him to handle it. I'd never let a heat go this far before. My dick ached like I'd been denying a release for months, and my hole clenched, sending needy spasms through my body. But, if I was going to trust Magnus implicitly from now on, then I might as well start now. I leaned back, my shoulders hitting the cool porcelain rim as my legs stretched out in front of me. My erection bobbed at the water line, and I whimpered.

"What's wrong? Are you hurting?" Magnus asked.

"No, it's just that it feels… so much."

"You act as if you've never gone into a full heat before," Magnus said as he dipped the bar of soap into the bathwater before working it into a lather between his hands.

I didn't respond because I couldn't get my tongue to work like that and because I didn't want to lie.

My silence didn't go unnoticed, though.

"How could you have never experienced a full heat? Even the richest omegas must endure it. Unless they have some shady alpha who can—"

He stopped speaking, and I assumed that was the moment he'd caught on.

"How can a pimp afford suppressors for—"

"I don't want to talk about him right now," I said, launching my upper half out of the tub, ready to take what I needed instead of waiting for it. That thought made me pause. Was that what went through an alpha's head?

I didn't have to keep wondering, though, because Magnus settled into the space beside the tub and grabbed my hand, massaging my fingers and palm. At first, I wanted to complain and ask when we would get to the good stuff, but I laid back instead, closed my eyes, and let him do what he wanted.

It didn't take long for me to settle into a hazy state of comfort, like I was suspended in that space between awake and asleep, disrupted only when Magnus needed to create more lather, or when he moved to the other hand where he continued the massage, working up my arm as well. He moved to my shoulders next, soothing away the tension.

When he moved down to the other half, I expected my body to react, but an odd thing happened while he massaged. I let go. Let myself become this weightless thing suspended in water, massaged by loving hands. I could still feel the heat symptoms, but only the good ones. None of the pain or violent longing.

That didn't mean that when his hands finally slid to the inside of my thighs that I wasn't ready. But Magnus did not waver from his plan. He massaged the soft flesh of my inner legs, moving slowly upward. When his fingers brushed against my crack, I jerked, splashing water over the edge of the tub. "You're doing so well," he crooned as he rubbed. "Heats don't have to be scary. You can even learn to enjoy your heat—if you have the right partner."

I opened my eyes. His face was close to mine, and I smiled. "I do."

His kiss was everything I'd been hoping for. His tongue was gentle yet insistent, and when his hands cupped my face, they trembled. I peeked down at his lap, spotted the impressive bulge, and realized that everything I was going through happened to him as well. Heats worked both ways. While it started in my body, the pheromones I gave off started a chain reaction in him. His wolf was probably howling at him to bend me over the tub and get it over with. And yet he refused. For me.

I growled into his mouth and wrapped my arms around his neck. He lifted me from the water, not caring that I was getting him wet. He grabbed a towel, wiping my legs and arms dry before setting me back down on the bed. I sighed into the cushioned warmth, turning into Magnus when he joined me after stripping.

His skin felt like a furnace, and his cock was like an iron pole between us. He pulled me close, encouraging me to wrap and twist around him until I wasn't sure where my body stopped and his started. He let his hand slide down my ass crack as we kissed, and he tickled my pucker, making me gasp.

My body offered little resistance as he probed with one finger, pushing into the first knuckle before stopping and kissing me deeply. He pushed further, reaching the second knuckle and then all the way. I moaned, leaning back into his hand like I was taking a seat. "It's never felt like this before," I murmured against his skin as he continued to fuck me with his finger. My balls tightened, and my cock jerked before releasing a stream of creamy fluid. "Oh my God, Magnus!" I wailed out his name as I came, but he never stopped kissing or fondling. A moment later, I felt a second finger joining the first. My ass muscles gripped onto it, drawing him in my body while remaining reluctant to let him go.

"I love hearing my name when you say it like that," he whispered, fucking me fervently with two fingers. "You growl when you come, tiny angry, sexy bursts of noise."

I hadn't realized that was something I did, but now that he pointed it out, I heard it. I pressed my lips to his as he kept thrusting, stretching me out, making me feel pleasure with just his hands and mouth. I could lay there like that forever, used and fondled by my alpha. But, his desire kept pressing into my stomach, thick, hot, and ready. I salivated and tried to bend over to get a taste of him. I already knew I liked the flavor.

But he stopped me. "I'm fine, babe. Just let me tend to you."

He pulled away then, grabbing my legs and dragging them toward the foot of the bed so that I laid flat on the mattress. He sat between my legs, using a pillow to prop up my lower half, putting both my cock and asshole on display.

"If this isn't the most beautiful sight in the world..." he murmured, taking a moment to simply stare at my body. He pushed a finger into my hole, and it went in easily as he opened his mouth and enveloped my erection in his moist heat.

A kaleidoscope of colors burst on the ceiling as I stared

upward and screamed. I could feel every swipe of his hot tongue, every centimeter of his finger dragging over my nerve endings. My ass clenched over his finger, quickly coming to the conclusion that it wasn't enough—I needed more. And yet, when he crooked the finger inside of me, making a beckoning gesture, I came so hard my voice gave out halfway through, allowing nothing more than airy gasps to escape.

If this was what it felt like to be manhandled, I couldn't imagine what it would feel like to get fucked while in heat.

But I knew I needed it. Any other time that I had been turned on before this moment suddenly paled in comparison. I felt more like my wild wolf counterpart than I did like a man. I was ready to pin him back and crawl on top of him when he suddenly growled.

"I can't hold back any longer," he said apologetically.

He'd been trying to hold back?

I slipped out from under his upper half and turned over, drawing my knees up to hold my body while I braced my hands against the headboard. I looked over my shoulder and wiggled my ass. "Then don't."

Magnus roared as he launched forward. For a split second, I almost didn't recognize his face until he found my eyes. This was Magnus, a man who had quickly carved a space for himself in my heart. I didn't need to be afraid. He wouldn't hurt me. I thrust my ass back, a silent invitation that he was completely ready to accept.

His dick was engorged and flushed nearly purple. Pre-cum leaked from his bulbous head, and while I would've loved a taste, I needed his girth inside of me.

Magnus didn't make me wait.

He flexed his hips forward, sheathing his length completely in a single thrust. I threw my head back and wailed as my body clenched around him. Now that it had gotten what it wanted, it wasn't going to give it up. Magnus's moans dissolved into groans and then just growls as he thrust forward, again and again. He filled me to the brim, only to empty me almost completely again. Sometime during this, I came again, only aware of it when Magnus brought his cum-covered fingers to my lips. "Taste yourself, omega. Taste why you're making me crazy," he grunted, and I opened my lips, tasting and swallowing my essence.

Magnus liked that very much, if the pace of his thrusts were any indication. I clung to the headboard, my legs shaking as I thrust my ass out and up. I felt his dick swelling the moment before his growls changed, growing deeper and longer.

"Yes!" I screamed, delirious with the need to feel his knot.

Magnus snarled, thrusting deeper than he had before, breaking through any barrier I'd put up between us in the process. His dick grew, swelling to keep him in place as he delivered his seed. He made the motions of thrusting, even though he could no longer move easily in and out. His teeth found my shoulder, and he bit, licking the spot while growling, "My hole, this is my hole. Mine."

If any other alpha in the world had said something like that to me, they would've walked away minus a dick—if they were lucky. But from Magnus, I couldn't agree more.

I was his.

CHAPTER NINE
Magnus

My omega walked out of the bathroom, the plumes of steam framing him from behind. I balanced my head on my hand, lying sideways on the bed so that I could watch every sensuous sway. He smirked, fully aware of the effect he had on me. I couldn't pinpoint the exact moment he'd changed toward me. Sometime after meeting my parents, maybe. But he had changed. His touches lingered longer, and he smiled a little brighter, as if he'd been wavering on the edge of a decision that he'd finally made.

As long as his decisions brought him closer to me, I'd be happy. I'd already started constructing a plan for when we went back. First, I'd need to be able to formally extricate him from whatever bound him to the alpha he lived with. I wouldn't ask that he immediately bind himself to me, but I would make sure that he was protected.

"Are you sure your heat is ebbing?" I asked, cupping his hip as he came close enough. "We don't have to leave yet."

He paused in the act of drying his hair. His golden eyes seemed to glow in the dimly lit room. "But you told your friends you'd meet them. Unless... you don't want me to go?"

A growl bubbled from me as I snagged him around the waist and pulled him so that he straddled my middle. He was still naked, which meant I got an awesome view. "You missed my objective there, which was to stay here with you, not go without."

"Oh!" Wynn replied with a smile. This close, his eyes looked like the wispy flames of a fire. "I'm okay with staying, but we don't have to because of my heat. I was feeling better before the last time, and then *after* I was feeling really good."

True to his word, his cock remained soft, but no less appealing. I gazed at the body part in question, grinning as he grew hard before my eyes.

"You can't blame me when you look at it like that! And unless you think there is a cause for me to have my dick out in your view while we hang with your friends—"

This growl was less of a bubble and more of a statement. "No. That will not be happening. I'm old fashioned in some ways, Wynn. Sharing you is one of them." No use in sugar coating it. If he had a problem with this, then we had a long conversation ahead. One where I would convince him that he was mine and mine alone.

"I like that more than I thought I would," Wynn replied.

I leaned forward and sniffed. I could detect only faint hints of his heat pheromone, not much more than what would be there most other days of the month. I was eager to get to the pub—not just to meet back up with the alphas I'd wasted many an hour with, but to introduce Wynn to my world. From what I'd seen, my world was much different from the one he'd experienced growing up, and I wanted to show him what it was like to live in a community like South Side, where people looked out for one another. "Maybe we should have sex one more time," I suggested.

Wynn laughed and slipped from on top of me and out of my hold at the same time. Every once in awhile, he showed me a glimpse of this other omega. One that moved impossibly quick and who made me believe he only *let* me grab and hold onto him. "I think at this point more sex will have a negative effect."

I understood his hesitation. After the first round the night before, we'd had sex basically the entire night that followed, taking small nap breaks between sessions. The morning had brought us back to my parents' house until my endless growling at anyone who walked by the sidewalk out front made my omega dad insist I take Wynn back to the hotel for my own peace of mind. We'd continued the sleep-sex schedule until the afternoon, when Pat called saying a bunch of them were meeting up at Jimmy's.

The last time we had sex, my knot didn't produce, a clear sign that Wynn's heat had been satisfied. That didn't mean he was pregnant. It only meant his body's sensors had detected my knot and seed often enough to be relieved. Pregnancy was just a possible side effect, not the actual goal.

"I just want you to feel comfortable wherever we go," I said, standing to cup his face and give him a gentle kiss.

"As long as you're there," he replied, making me feel like the luckiest man in the world.

I left him in the room long enough to shower. At dusk we were dressed. I didn't plan on drinking so we drove to Jimmy's pub.

Walking through the lopsided entrance was like walking into the past. Memories flooded in, nights spent nursing pints because none of us ever had much money. Then there were the nights earlier than that, when not one of us could've been older than twelve or so, sent down by someone's omega dad to go pick up their alpha dad who had indulged a little too much. After a few years, our little pack got so good at dragging people home that Jimmy used to call our gang even if the drunk in question wasn't related to any of us.

We never minded. In fact, we all got a sense of pride

helping. South Siders took care of each other.

"Big dog!" Terrance's voice boomed my old nickname first, starting a chorus of the same.

"Big dog!"

"Big dog!"

Terrance, Clipper, Pat, and Fang waved at us from a table in the far corner. Jimmy's wasn't a fancy place. The only window was near the entrance. The rest was dark, dingy, and hadn't been redecorated since it opened. The walls lined with wood paneling and decorated with old neon signs that advertised the types of beer and liquor they'd had available through the years.

"Those are your friends?" Wynn whispered, his steps slower than they'd been walking in.

I gestured to the table to give us a second and pulled Wynn closer to the wall. "Are you okay with all of this?"

"Of course," he said without looking at me. When his face turned my direction, he smiled. "I'm completely fine, *big dog*."

I snorted. "We were kids. What did you expect, *original* nicknames? Didn't you have something similar with your pals, omegas you grew up with?"

Wynn gave me one of those sly smiles he sometimes had, making me think I'd told the punchline of an inside joke I wasn't a part of. "Something like that, yes. C'mon, I want to meet your friends."

I grabbed his hand, loving the way he squeezed it before settling warmly at my side.

Where he belonged.

As we neared again, the chorus started once more. "Big dog!"

"Hey, guys," I called out, giving one-armed hugs over the table. "I can't believe you're all still here."

"Was that a burn?" Clipper stage-whispered to Pat.

"I think it was. Translation, why didn't you all abandon your home, friends, and family to become a bigshot in the city?" Pat said.

Beside me, Wynn growled. I squeezed his hand. "It was nothing like that, and you know it," I replied with a smile.

"Yeah, you guys know why he had to leave," Terrance said.

"I'm just teasing," Pat said, raising his hands. "Call off your mate."

I looked to Wynn to see if he had a problem with the term. His cheeks were pink, but his lips were smiling. "You definitely don't want him on your bad side," I said, unable to keep myself from leaning over and kissing him on the tip of his nose. An action that only made the rest of the guys at the table groan. "Guys, meet Wynn. I told him you were upstanding, trustworthy alphas, so don't go and prove me wrong."

"Why would you lie to your mate like that?" Terrance asked while reaching out for Wynn's hand. Wynn gave him the one I wasn't holding, and Terrance brought it to his lips. I'd forgotten how much of a damn flirt he was. "Pleasure to meet the man capable of getting Magnus to look away from his work."

"I wouldn't want to do that," Wynn replied softly. "Magnus's work is important."

That triggered a second round of groans that transformed into teasing before moving into what everyone was up to these days. Sometime during that, the guys ordered a few pitchers, not blinking twice when Wynn ordered a water and I ordered an iced tea.

I discovered that Clipper and Pat both worked in South Side at their family businesses, the mart on the corner and the butcher's, respectively. Fang's piece of shit dad had finally died, leaving him in charge of running the house. He still had an omega brother at home and going to school. I couldn't believe Fang's brother was in high school now—he'd been a little boy when I'd left. And Terrance was now a police officer, patrolling the same streets he used to loiter.

"The power is getting to his head," Clipper grumbled.

"Do you know he tried to give me a parking ticket?"

"You had your junker double-parked for three days," Terrance said.

Clipper just gave me an *are you seeing this* expression. Then the look on Clipper's face soured as a shadow appeared on our table, coming from behind Wynn.

I turned to find the figure responsible, barely concealing a growl when I saw the culprit standing a few feet away on Wynn's side.

"Fancy businessman comes home?" Veryl snarled. Time had not been good to him. Granted, the last time I'd seen him he'd been a young man, coming into his status as an alpha. He'd been snarling at me and telling me all the ways he would kill me for what I did to his brother.

That had been what had made me the angriest, that Veryl had been mad for what *I'd* done to *his* brother while his brother had killed mine.

"Get the fuck out of here, man," Fang said, moving to get to his feet. I put my hand on his shoulder to stop him. I didn't want this turning ugly in front of Wynn.

"Veryl, I can't say it is good to see you," I said.

Veryl snarled. He had beady black eyes that were too close together and bushy black eyebrows that only exaggerated that fact. His lips were thin and pale, like he spent all his time pressing them together. Behind him, he had a pack of men. Some I recognized. Others I didn't. They all looked angry.

"This is Veryl?" Wynn asked, his voice cold. He must've remembered that this was the little brother to the alpha who had murdered Matty. The one currently rotting in prison for the rest of his life.

"My brother's getting out, you know." Veryl let the words ooze out of his mouth.

The blood from my face drained to my fists, making them feel red hot and me murderous. "That's impossible. He got life—"

"With the possibility of parole," Veryl snapped. "And

he's been in prison for more than fifteen years. More than enough time to atone for any—"

My pulse pounded in my ears. "He murdered my brother."

"The omega slut?" Veryl replied.

Everyone at our table stood, but I was quick to wave them down. "We're here to catch up, and you're a cop now, Terrance. You all have responsibilities and families. Don't jeopardize any of that for me. Especially not for this sad sack of shit." I shouldn't have said it, but I wasn't a saint, and the fact that I wasn't snapping his arms in two should've been cause enough to make me one.

"Yeah guys," Veryl said to his group, mocking my tone while inserting a nasal quality that I was sure I didn't have. "Don't break your fingernails pretending to be alphas."

The guys at my table snarled but remained still.

Veryl looked down his crooked, greasy nose at Wynn. "Why don't you do yourself a favor and find a real alpha to satisfy you?"

Wynn didn't look at him when he replied. "Why don't you do yourself a favor and take a bath?"

The guys at my table laughed. Even I smirked—until Veryl grabbed Wynn by his left wrist.

I got to my feet, but Wynn moved too quickly for any of us to intervene. With his right, he yanked on Veryl's arm, tugging his own wrist free and pulling Veryl's arm straight out in front of his body in the process. In the second half of that same instant, Wynn whipped his left hand forward toward Veryl's elbow. I couldn't follow the impact clearly but heard a sharp snap.

Veryl hollered in pain the next moment and the place exploded with movement. The alphas at my table all stood, facing off against Veryl's pack. They had rushed forward snarling and growling, some of them shifting while others unveiled various weapons.

Veryl had been planning for this to be a party.

Except now his back was to Wynn. Veryl's broken arm

hung at an unnatural angle as he howled, going silent when Wynn brought a steak knife up to his throat—one that he must've swiped from the table, but God only knew when.

"Get out of here, or your friend won't just lose his ability to jack-off for a few weeks," Wynn said calmly. Like he hadn't just broken a man's arm and was now threatening to slice his throat. His eyes shone, alive and focused.

Those in wolf form were the first to turn tail and run out the door. I watched them leave out of the corner of my eye, noticing every patron in the place had stopped what they were doing to just stare at Wynn. I understood. None of them had ever seen an omega raise his voice, much less defend himself in such a public setting.

But most of Veryl's group had remained, causing Wynn to snarl and press the serrated edge of the knife further into Veryl's skin. "Do you think I'm joking?" he asked as a trickle of blood escaped from under the blade.

"Wynn," I said, reaching out for him while the rest of Veryl's friends put down their weapons. All but two walked calmly out of Jimmy's.

"He deserves worse than this, Magnus," Wynn replied, and I could honestly say I didn't recognize the tone. He didn't sound like the quietly serious man I knew, or even the proud yet playful version. This was someone else, someone I'd never met.

"Not like this, not here," I told him, unsure of what my omega was going to do next.

"Just let us take him home. We won't come back. We promise," one of Veryl's friends said with more respect than he'd ever spoken to an omega in his life.

A tense second passed. Then Wynn dropped the knife and shoved Veryl away. "You're alive because Magnus commanded it. Remember that."

Veryl's friends gathered him, propping him up under the armpits with their shoulders. They dragged him out in that way. The door swung softly shut behind him, leaving the rest of us in stunned silence.

"What," Terrance began.

"The fuck," Clipper added.

"Was that?" Pat said.

Fang pumped his fist over his head. "That was fucking awesome! I knew you had to be special if you were with this guy, but fucking hell, Magnus, where did you find him and does he have a brother?" He stood tall and then narrowed his eyes at the table. "You're alive because Magnus commanded it," he said, imitating Wynn's emotionless tone. "Fuck, man, that gave me the shivers. And a chub."

"Fang," I warned.

"Sorry, man, but you're…" He let out a low whistle. "So fucking lucky."

The rest of my friends seemed to share Fang's sentiment. In fact, the entire rest of the bar had to come over, congratulating Wynn—from a safe distance—while clapping me on the back.

Wynn took it in stride, even started smiling some toward the end. But I couldn't shake the feeling that he'd become someone I didn't know during those tense minutes. "Where did you learn how to do that?" I asked between pats on the back and offers to buy the table drinks.

"You taught me self-defense, remember?" Wynn replied, accepting a basket of fries while refusing a tray of suspiciously purple shots.

"I didn't teach you that."

Wynn shrugged. "You gave me the foundation. I guess the rest just builds on top pretty easily."

"Why are you questioning that display of fucking awesomeness?" Terrance asked. "Come show me the move, Wynn. I'll impress the guys at the station tomorrow."

Wynn looked to me, and I nodded, the whole time watching him move and wondering if I really knew my omega at all.

CHAPTER TEN
Wynn

Magnus didn't speak during the drive back to the hotel from Jimmy's. We'd stayed long enough for all the food people had bought us to arrive. I ate as much as I could, and Magnus said the rest should be shared, since everyone had been pretty drunk by that point.

What I'd done had been a hit—pun unintended—with everyone but Magnus, who kept shooting me secretive glances from the bed. He'd turned on the television but didn't look at it for more than five seconds at a time before looking my way.

Meanwhile, I wasn't sure what I'd done wrong. Veryl was an alphahole who had deserved two broken arms. I'd stopped at one. Didn't that count for anything?

"At least we don't have to worry about dinner," I said rising from where I'd been sitting on the chair at the small desk in our room. Even though my heat had subsided, I thought about taking advantage of the second room. Learning how to navigate a happy relationship had been hard enough. I had no idea how to do whatever this was. "I'm sorry if I made you upset earlier. I remembered that guy from the story you told me about Matty, and he was being so horrible—"

"I'm not mad at that. Veryl deserved what he got. I just didn't want anyone to get into trouble because of it. Or you getting hurt in the process. But I guess I don't need to worry about that, do I?"

He definitely didn't say that like he was happy for the fact. But why would he want me to be helpless?

"Should I have sat there and let him manhandle me like a good omega?" I bit out.

Magnus blinked rapidly, turning my direction. "No, of course not. I just…I don't know how a hoo—someone who grew up doing what you did knows how to move like that. That wasn't the result of a few self-defense classes. That was *years* of training. It's unusual, Wynn."

Someone who grew up doing what I did? Oh yeah, he thought I was a long-term prostitute. I could understand how he would've come to that conclusion when he first saw me all those years ago, but it hurt that he could've spent so much time with me and still thought me capable of that. To him, a hooker was a victim, an omega that had sunk the lowest to survive. Didn't he see that no one touched me without me wanting it? On the heels of that thought was another, equally dangerous. Did he understand the type of person I was at all? Not what I did for a living, but who I was at my core? Had I ever given him an opportunity? This whole time, I thought it was me Magnus was following in love with, but was it really my mission's persona all along?

Because if he was angry about what had happened today, then he would be angry again, and soon. Leaving the OAC had never meant turning myself into a meek mouse. We lived in a world where my body was a free space, like the center square on a bingo card. He'd inked his stamp on me for now, but that wouldn't stop others from trying or me from setting their delusions straight. Sometimes violently.

"This feels a lot like you being angry that I defended myself."

Magnus sat up. The remote control fell from his chest to the bed. "How can you say that?"

I crossed my arms over my chest. "I can only come to conclusions using the evidence in front of me."

"You see, that, things like that." He stood and marched closer to me. "When you talk about evidence, or use a maneuver I've never even seen before, or say something that makes it seem like you live this life of crime and violence. How does what you did in the past explain all of that, Wynn? It doesn't."

Earlier that day, I'd been ready to give up my life at the OAC, my pack family and friends, for this suspicious alpha who wanted me to wait to be rescued rather than rescue myself? Except that wasn't who Magnus was. He had questions, I could at least try to answer them. "Our boss made sure we were prepared for any sort of—"

"That's bullshit," Magnus snarled, reaching back to scratch his neck. "I know when you're lying to me—"

"I doubt that," I shot back.

Magnus stood straight, mirroring me with crossed arms. "Wynn, I am not angry that you defended yourself. I'm upset that there was cause for you to at all. But I won't be lied to. Not if you're going to be my mate."

Ouch. "I thought I already was." I centered my weight on the balls of my feet, wondering how many steps it would take me to get from this room to the room next to ours. Would Magnus try to stop me?

I didn't know what he saw in my expression or body language, but it was enough to make him sway back, lifting his hands in surrender. "Hold on, Wynn."

I reached down for the bag I'd packed. It had clothes that Magnus had let me borrow and the disassembled pieces of my phone, but I hugged it to my front. "Maybe I should sleep in the other room tonight."

"You can, if that's what you want. I'm not here to control you. I just want answers. I just want to know who you are. How come that is such a big issue? It isn't unreasonable for me to want to know my mate, is it?"

"You do know me. The parts that matter the most, anyway."

"Then where did you learn that? What you did at the bar? That was some action movie stuff."

I'd tried to give him the acceptable answer. It was twice removed from the truth, but when the truth was *I was hired to kill you, and you weren't the first, not by a long shot*, how could anyone expect me to bare my soul? Maybe he could forgive what happened today, but how could he forgive what I'd done? It had been for a purpose, a cause I still believed in, but I could hardly forgive myself. Most days, I didn't, and I wouldn't give him any reason to look at me like I was a monster.

"I'm going to bed," I said, dropping my bag on the carpet by the bed while deciding I wouldn't run to the adjoined room. If this was Magnus's limit, then it was one we would've reached eventually. I'd already showered and dressed for bed so I slipped under the covers, turning away from him like a pouting child.

"Wynn, I want to talk about this. I just need to know—"

"Something I'm not willing to tell." I finished his sentence without rolling around. Why should I bare every dirty, horrible detail to him before I was ready, just to satisfy a curiosity? "Are you going to try to force the information out of me?" I said, immediately feeling as if I'd been gut-punched. Asking him that was a low blow that hurt us both.

Better we both hurt now than wait and worry. What had I planned on doing when he finally decided I really wasn't worth all the trouble? That having a mild, obedient omega really was preferable? Where was I supposed to go? I'd already secured a life where I'd mattered. My thoughts, feelings and emotions had been important to those around me. Until I'd shit on it—no better than that omega I'd scared away that first day I'd bumped into Magnus on his way to the bathroom.

"I can't believe you would even say that." His anguished tone tore chunks out of my heart.

I sighed sadly, tiredly. "You're right. I'm sorry. I'm going to bed before I say anything else I regret. I suggest you do the same."

I didn't roll over to see if he did as I said, but minutes later, I heard the squeak of the mattress, felt it shake around as he got into bed. He didn't pull me to him or say a word, but at least he was there still. I couldn't go back to the OAC. By now, I was officially AWOL, which meant I could be subjected to any punishment that Taft saw fit. After our last conversation, I shuddered to think what that punishment would be. I swore to myself the moments before a fitful sleep came that I would make up for this tomorrow. Not with the truth, because that was impossible, but somehow, I'd bring us back to the happy bubble we'd been in before my violence popped it.

CHAPTER ELEVEN
Magnus

It was around four in the morning when I gave up on sleeping entirely. As far as I could tell, Wynn slept soundly, but I didn't know how many of his actions I could believe anymore. He'd refused to tell me more about his past, though what bothered me the most was *how* he'd refused, like he was terrified of the truth.

When he'd gone to bed, I'd wanted to shake him awake and convince him that I only want to know for his safety. There wasn't anything he could say that would push me away. But if I wasn't going to do anything with the information he told me, then why did I want to know so badly? For my own edification? Or maybe because he already knew so much about me? I'd talked to him about Matty—something I never did. I even told him about my latest invention, something everyone else in the world had to sign an NDA before hearing a single word.

I wasn't asking him to do anything that I hadn't been willing to do myself, which only made his reasons more suspicious. From the moment Wynn had gone to sleep, I'd had time to come up with any and every possible scenario,

123

but now, as the sun began to warm up the horizon, I was sure it had to be because Wynn was in danger.

From what? Or who?

I would just have to find out.

I told myself it was for Wynn's safety when I slipped out of bed and crept around to the other side where Wynn had dropped his bag. Before I could change my mind, I grabbed the handle and rushed around to the bathroom, shutting the door and turning on the exhaust as I pulled out the pieces of Wynn's phone.

Back at my penthouse, my weird alarm had first gone off when I walked out of the shower to find Wynn saying we should just get away while hastily shoving the disassembled parts of his cell out of my view. I'd figured that he didn't want to be able to be contacted, but now, I needed to know who he was hiding from.

I looked up at the door, waiting for a moment to listen to Wynn's breaths. They were even and relaxed.

My wolf growled at me, unhappy with my actions, but to him life was about claiming and possessing and protecting. He should know that what I was doing was for Wynn's own good. That didn't stop his snarling, but I ignored it, slipping the identity module pack into place first. I set the phone on the edge of the sink, staring at it for a span of time that could've been seconds or hours. I could still turn back, replace everything how I'd found it, and go back to sleep. But if Wynn wasn't going to tell me what was after him, then I had to find out myself. I clicked the battery back in and powered the phone on.

It took it a whole thirty seconds before it rang. The number was blocked, but the caller ID read only a number one instead of a contact name. I answered.

"What the fuck do you think you're doing?" a deep voice snarled on the other end.

"Who are you?" I barked back. I could tell just by the other man's tone that he was an alpha. Was this Wynn's pimp?

There was only silence for a moment, and then, "Is my omega alive?"

I growled at the possessive term. "He's asleep right now."

The alpha on the line let out a growl identical to my own. The back of my neck began to itch.

"Is he hurt?" the alpha asked.

"I would never hurt Wynn. You're the one who thrusts him into unsafe environments. Do you even care that he's so young? Of course not. You started with him so long ago."

"I must be confused. Where is my omega, and what are you doing to him?" the man asked.

My entire body was tense. Something was wrong here, but I didn't know what. "Why do you think I am the one hurting him? You're the one selling his body for money."

The other man started to laugh. "You think Wynn is a prostitute? Is that what he told you or what you assumed?"

"It wasn't hard to figure out—"

"And he never bothered to contradict you either. Why would he when you made up his cover story for him?"

I paced the short length of the bathroom. "Look, I didn't turn on his phone to argue with you. I'm telling you that Wynn is done with that life. Whatever sort of life you gave him, he's done with it." I sat down on the edge of the tub.

The other alpha was quiet for a moment. "It's clear you care for him, Magnus. This is Magnus, right? He's talked about you. But, Wynn is sick. Not in his body—there he is in peak shape—but in his mind. Tell me where you are, and I'll bring him home. He should be nearing his heat. He needs to be someplace—"

"You don't have to worry about that," I replied, hating that this man knew my name. That meant Wynn had at least spoken about me with him. But, the man on the other end of the phone didn't sound like he was worried the way a boss worried for his employees, or even the way a father worried for his son. This felt more than that. Romantic.

I waited a full second longer before realizing he'd hung the phone up, immediately after I'd admitted to satisfying Wynn's heat.

"What are you doing with my phone?" Wynn asked sharply. He stood in the doorway. His hair stuck up in all angles, and his eyes were still clouded with sleep, but they were quickly clearing and narrowing at me.

I lifted my chin, feeling not even a fraction of the confidence I was projecting. "I needed answers."

Wynn made a noise that sounded like all the air had whooshed out of his body. He yanked the phone free and glanced at the screen. "You called Taft?" His voice grew both higher in pitch and lower in volume as his face paled. He jerked his face up, his eyes wide and round. "How long? How much time?"

"What? We spoke for a few seconds."

"No, Magnus. How long has the phone been on?"

I frowned and followed Wynn out of the bathroom. He shoved a shirt over his head, not seeming to care that it was both inside out and backwards.

"Minutes, if that. Why?"

Wynn ignored me, pacing back and forth in the room like a nervous hummingbird. I grabbed his elbow and held on when he tried to pull away. "What is going on? Is Taft your pimp?"

Wynn blinked. For a moment he looked lost. "You don't have any idea what you've done. But how could you?" He shook his head and backed away from me. His hair whipped against his cheek with every violent turn. "I did this. By not telling you enough to satisfy your concerns. You wanted to believe I was this other type of person, and I did nothing to dissuade you of that. Now, you can't trust me because you don't know me. This is why I'm so bad at these missions! I don't understand how people work." He paused, giving me an expression reminiscent of the one he'd had the night before while he'd held a knife to Veryl's throat. "I only understand how they die."

I growled on my inner wolf's urging. Just talking about death had him on edge, made him want to identify the enemy. "Do you think this Taft is coming here? Even if he is, we have hours."

"The OAC headquarters are between here and downtown. They're closer than you think. Especially if they take the jet."

If I thought he hadn't made sense before, I really didn't now. I'd never heard of anything called the OAC. And his casual talk of jets made my eyebrows dip into a V. "He said that you were sick, in your mind, Wynn…" Even if he was, there were doctors that could handle this, medicine he could take.

Wynn started laughing which really wasn't helping the whole sanity thing. "That *would* be what Taft told you. Smart, really, casts doubt on anything I've told you already while making you predisposed not to believe anything I say from this point on. Genius. The fucker."

"He's an alpha."

"Yeah," Wynn shot back with great sarcasm.

"Is he *your* alpha?"

Wynn froze in the act of shoving his phone back in the bag. His lips twisted in a sneer, but the whole thing seemed tinged in sadness. "Is that what you're still worried about? Who I belong to? I told you I was yours. That's all you should have to hear. But it isn't, is it? You wanted to hear from Taft that I was yours. You wanted to prove it. Well, congrats, he knows about us now."

"I won't be a dirty secret—"

"That's *never* what you were." His hands shook. The vibrations traveled up his spine until his entire body trembled. With his wide, fear-filled eyes and baggy borrowed clothes, he finally looked the frightened omega I'd expected him to be from the first day.

And it terrified me.

"Were?" I asked.

He shook his head, backing away from me. "I can't stay here."

Behind him, there was a knock on the door. Then solid, even raps.

Wynn sunk into a defensive crouch, whirling toward the door as if he was going to protect me from whatever was on the other side. "I thought you said you'd only put the phone together a few minutes ago?" Wynn rasped out of the corner of his mouth.

"I did… I… put the chip in, but some time passed while I was thinking of my next steps. Wait, are you saying they tracked us? There wasn't even power to the unit."

"There's always residual energy stored. The chip needed a fraction of that to send our location."

The knock sounded again, followed by, "I know you're in there." The voice sounded exactly like the man who had been on the phone. "Not only did your friend allow me to triangulate your position, but I can hear you. Come on, sweetie, I'm just worried."

Wynn snorted, but I didn't know what to believe. My heart and wolf told me to grab Wynn and slip out through the bathroom window, but my head said that things hadn't added up the moment I bumped into Wynn for the second time. I moved toward the door, but Wynn grabbed my hand. "What are you doing?" he hissed.

"Getting answers, Wynn. I need them, or we won't work. We can't."

"And if you don't trust me, you'll die," Wynn replied.

My stomach clenched. Was he threatening me? Or was the threat on the other side of the door?

"Sweetheart, you don't need to be so dramatic," Taft called through the door. "I have the hotel worker with me here. He has a key, so either he can let me in or you can. But I will be bringing you home. River, Van, and Zed are over the moon worried for you."

"Who are they?" I asked. "Are they your friends? Your children?"

Outside, Taft made a noise like a barking laugh. "He is really good at coming to his own conclusions, isn't he? River, Van, and Zed are three wolves who are very eager to have Wynn back in their lives. Mr. Gray, I know you just worry for Wynn. That's why I have to tell you. He's extremely sick, and without his medicine, he becomes violent. I'm sure you've seen a glimpse of his *odd behaviors*, or else you wouldn't have been fishing for answers."

My nape wouldn't stop itching, but I didn't know who was the one lying. I grabbed Wynn, pulling him close and cupping his chin so that he would look at me. "Tell me the truth. Who are you? I'll believe you, I promise. I just need you to *tell me*."

Wynn closed his eyes. His lip trembled. When his eyelashes lifted, they shimmered with tears. "And I needed you to wait until I was ready to give you that information. I was wrong. You're more like the typical alpha than I wanted to believe. You never forced me but you still ignored my wishes and went behind my back because you thought you knew better. And now I'm in a corner." Wynn pushed from me, reaching back and retrieving a knife that looked exactly like the one from Jimmy's the night before.

"You stole that?"

Wynn just rolled his eyes. "The thing about corners isn't that they trap you, it's that they give you only one way out." Without any further warning, he sprinted to the door, wrenching it open before leaping forward with a loud battle cry.

The man on the other side of the door seemed to be expecting such a maneuver because he stepped out of the way at the last minute, circling his thick arms around Wynn's slim frame and squeezing as the omega struggled.

I jerked forward.

"You've done enough, Mr. Gray, thank you. My name is Taft and my omega is very sick. If he takes his medicine, he can operate normally, but he claims he doesn't like how it makes him feel. I only want the best for him, you see. And I might have let him go a bit wild because of that. You've done a good thing."

I was five feet away, my hands clenched into tight fists while my fangs sharpened instinctively. My neck itched like crazy, and I was sure of only one thing. I'd made a mistake. "Wynn? What do *you* want?"

"Isn't it late to ask me that?" Wynn snarled his reply. He'd stopped fighting against Taft's hold, but the other alpha still had him pressed close.

That was hard enough to see. When Taft bent his head, whispering something in Wynn's ear that made Wynn's mouth pop into an O shape, I could barely stand watching.

"My omega wants to return with me," Taft said next, loud enough for me to hear.

"What did he just say to you?" I asked, taking another step forward.

Wynn wouldn't look at me. He stood slumped, his head ducked between his shoulders and his face toward the ground. "He said I'm leaving, and you're staying. And that's... that's how I want it." His voice broke at the end.

"You're lying, Wynn. I'm calling the cops."

"No!" Wynn's face jerked up to me, his face as afraid as I'd ever seen him. "Don't. He's right. I need my medicine and to return to my pack. Goodbye. Don't try to find me."

The two of them turned and headed toward the parking lot. I rushed out, coming to a stuttering stop at the helicopter that was parked in the middle of the cracked black asphalt. The blades whirred silently, indicating it had to be military-grade or higher.

The blades made a little more noise after Taft climbed in behind Wynn. But even then, it was a soft whooshing that brought the helicopter into the sky and took my mate away from me. I couldn't see Wynn as the helicopter disappeared on the horizon, but I knew that I'd fucked things up.

The only thing to do next was to fix it.

CHAPTER TWELVE
Wynn

"Oh good, you got the stray," Nolan sneered as the helicopter took off.

Though I wanted to slam his nose into the back of his brain, I didn't move. I was too afraid that Taft would go back on the threat he'd whispered in my ear at the exact moment I'd spotted Nolan's laser sight on Magnus's forehead. *Come now or I kill him.* I hadn't doubted him at that moment, and I didn't doubt him now. If Nolan so much as breathed in the direction of Magnus and the hotel, I'd push us both out the other side of the helicopter. The idiot wasn't wearing his safety harness. Like always.

But once we were too far for even his assault rifle to accurately shoot, I ignored Nolan and turned to Taft. "I want it in writing. You swore not to hurt him. I want that in writing."

Taft put his phone away after tapping on the screen, likely sending the message that I'd been retrieved. Though it had only been days since I'd last saw him, it looked more like weeks. He hadn't shaved. His dark brown beard covered the lower half of his face, while his eyes were bloodshot like he hadn't slept either. "Do you really think now is the time for you to be making demands? You're in deep shit, Wynn. Not just with me either. There are people above me, you know. I'm just the director. The founders are pissed. They want me to make an example out of you. This is their nightmare, for their agents to go rogue—"

Taft grabbed the collar of my shirt and yanked me toward him. His face was centimeters from mine. "No, you went AWOL. I didn't know if you'd been killed or if you were actively dying. You left like everything was fine. Leaving me to scramble for something to tell the founders. Do you even care that I managed to get them off your back? That they've agreed to let me punish you?"

"What? Are you going to whip me?"

Taft's face was ruddy with anger. "I should. In fact, I should just call back the founders and tell them you are beyond help. They'll send a cleaning crew to pick you up, deal with Magnus, and then I can—"

"No! You said he'd be safe if I left."

For some reason, that just made Taft angrier. He held my shirt so tightly the fabric dug into the back of my neck. I grew aware of the way my body had fallen, splayed over the top of his. "You've been doing missions for years without an issue. Other omegas need weeks after each mission with the psychologists, but you never do. You finish a job and immediately salivate for the next. What is it about this alpha? What does he have?"

I scowled. "A really big dick."

Nolan snorted, but Taft's forehead swung toward me, slamming into my face and turning off all the lights.

***

When I came to, I knew right away where I was, but not what had brought me here. It wasn't the first time I'd woken up in the infirmary. But it was the first time I'd woken up in handcuffs. I blinked, pain pounding in my head like a metronome keeping the beat.

"He's awake!" a soft, melodic voice called out.

"River?"

My packmate's round, angelic face came into view, his mouth turned down in the edges as the corners of his eyes wrinkled with worry. "Hey, you. We were worried."

I swallowed, trying to get the fuzz out of my head, but it was so hard when it pounded as loudly as it was. "What happened? How long have I been here?" Of all the times to pass out.

Then I remembered my last awake moments. Taft had headbutted me.

"You've been home for an hour," Zed said. I had to crane to see him standing in the corner with his arms crossed. "Why didn't you tell us you were sick of the OAC? We would have helped you petition to retire. But you just left us. When Taft stormed in asking where you were, none of us had any idea. River cried."

"Don't tell him that!" River squealed. "He'll feel worse than he already does." River turned, facing me again. "You do feel bad, right? For leaving us?"

I tried to reach for his hand, but the cuff wouldn't let me. "I never meant to leave you. It just…happened. The OAC is your life—"

"It was yours too. Until this mission," Van snapped, speaking for the first time.

"Look, you guys. This is… it's bigger than me, I think. My last target, Magnus, he wasn't at all the type of alpha Taft said he was. He's good and does work to help omegas."

"A bad guy doesn't have to be bad all the time to still be bad. The worst villains still donate to charities because it's tax-deductible," Van snarled. "I can't believe you let

him get into your head. You know what, no. I blame me.
And Zed and even River."

"Hey!" Zed and I both said.

River just dropped his head into his hands.

Van shook his head like he was waving away our
outcry. "No, it's on all of us. Nolan has never wanted to be
part of a pack. He's a lone wolf, which is why he always
butts heads, but the rest of us should have known. We
should have sensed it."

I shook my head slowly. "No. I refuse to accept that.
I'm not confused about the situation. You say you are my
pack brothers, so listen to me when I say that there is
something wrong with this mission. There was from the
very beginning. There may even be something wrong with
all of the OAC—"

The door opened, and Taft entered, followed by Nolan
who just sneered at the four of us. He was really loving
this. I was less concerned with Nolan's jubilance, though,
and more focused on what I spotted in Taft's hand. "What
is that?" My voice shook, clue enough for the other three
to stare at his hand.

River gasped.

"You've left me with little choice," Taft replied, though
something about him seemed entirely too pleased for that
to ring true. "I'm glad your team is here to see this.
Understand not only is it for your own good, but it is what
the founders have demanded." He came to the side of the
bed, setting the studded collar on the night table before
reaching for the cuffs at my wrists. He unlocked one,
leaned over my body, and unlocked the other.

I rubbed at the red skin.

Taft didn't move from my side. "Get up. Shift. I'll fit
this on you after."

"What is that?" Van asked.

"His collar. You should all hear this now anyway. Wynn is being grounded. For his safety and the safety of everyone at the OAC, he will be in his wolf form. He will wear this collar that will not only track his location but will inhibit him from being able to shift back. With this on, I'll know if he tries to step a single paw off the OAC campus."

He raised his hand, having to yell to be heard over my team's protests. "I understand that this may seem unorthodox, but Wynn's actions have allowed me no other recourse. His belongings will be moved into my home, where he will remain under my care until such a time I believe him to understand what it was that he's done wrong."

"An open-ended punishment based on your sole discretion?" Van asked. River and Zed took position on either side of him.

"Did Remington approve of this?" Zed asked.

"Remington is a beta and your team's handler. How well has he handled you all so far?"

Zed blushed, but lifted his chin stubbornly. "He trusts us when we are in the field."

"And look what has happened," Taft replied. To me, he added, "Shift, or I will make you shift."

There were chemical compounds that could induce shifting, but the process was unnatural and said to cause extreme pain. I pushed the white sheet down, unsurprised by my nudity. I noticed the way Taft stared at my body, like the dinner he'd ordered had just arrived.

I shifted, not enjoying the transformation as I normally would. I was almost entirely black in this form, a rarity among wolves since so many of us were fully bi or tri-colored. I did have a burst of white on my chest. My fur was normally glossy and smooth, but right now, it looked dull—reflecting how I felt on the inside.

I knew with every fiber of my being that this was wrong. Forcing me to shift was wrong. Demanding I stay that way to weaken me was wrong. But there was nothing I could do about it. Not without getting my team in danger because I could see it in their expressions. They were a breath away from fighting.

I shook my head at Van, hoping he could understand what I could no longer say.

"The rest of you will go. You still have training," Taft said. I stood stock-still as Taft worked the leather collar around my throat, locking it closed. Three inches from the buckle was a small plastic casing. Whatever technology it housed buzzed just loud enough for me to detect the sound.

The collar smelled strongly of Taft's scent, and I wondered how long he'd had the collar in his possession. It smelled only of him, so I didn't have to worry about him having used it on some other omega victim. I imagined Taft sitting alone in his room, holding the collar, stroking the stitching softly as he worked out a plan of getting it around my neck.

Had this been what he'd wanted all along?

"Even in that form, I can hear your voice," Taft murmured. "Don't worry. I'll help you heal. You won't be like this for long."

I turned my head away, looking to my team instead. That hadn't answered my question at all. My team was filing out of the room, leaving me alone.

I laid down, resting my head between my front paws. In the next moment, I felt tugging at my neck. Taft held a leather leash in the same material as the collar. He pulled on it, forcing me to my feet and then off the bed. "I still have work to do. You'll accompany me."

We walked out of the infirmary and down the hall. It was the middle of the day. Recruits were training, going

137

from class to class. Graduates were switching between working on missions and honing their skills. The halls weren't empty, and everyone stared as we passed by. Most whispered. I didn't care. I couldn't see them through my worry.

At Taft's office, he shut the door, leading me to the desk where he motioned for me to lay down underneath. I lifted my lip and growled. "Even now, you are so headstrong," Taft said with a grin. "Fine. You can lay here at my feet beside me."

Many things were becoming clear to me. One, Taft was not a friend of omegas. Two, the clients who had put the hit out on Magnus didn't give a fuck about omegas either. Three, when I got the chance, I was going to piss in Taft's shoes.

I stalled my plans for urine revenge when Taft cleared his throat and said, "I guess you should know and work on getting the tantrum over with. I've reassigned an omega to Magnus's case. The clients still want him dealt with. Only now they say the sooner the better."

I cocked my head to the side. If I hadn't already known the hit on Magnus had never been about the tech, I would know for sure now. Visadore must've been getting desperate to have Magnus gone as soon as possible.

I needed to get to him.

Taft chuckled. "I really can read you like a book. You're welcome. I know you appreciate that I can make the tough choices for you."

The hair down my spine stood straight up as I raised my hackles and growled. Again, that wasn't what I'd been thinking.

"Hey now, none of that. I kept my promise to you, Wynn. I said I wouldn't kill him. And as much as I want to kill him for thinking he could own you, I'm a man of my word. You really should be thanking me."

FERVOR

That was when I thanked Taft, biting into his thigh until I felt bone.

CHAPTER THIRTEEN
Wynn

My jaw hurt, and I wondered if I had a concussion an hour after Taft had beat me off his leg with his stapler. The growling and shouts had made so much noise that several OAC agents had rushed in. Each time, Taft waved off their worry with a different excuse. To some, he told, I was a traitor. To others, he told, I was taking part in a behavioral therapy experiment.

What he never did was tell the same story to more than a few people. Didn't he worry that they'd talk and their stories wouldn't add up? Or did he understand how gossip around these things tended to work? Every agent would turn right around and tell their team what they heard. The stories wouldn't mesh, but they'd be close enough that the more discerning would assume the changes in the story from person to person was human error or slight fabrication. No one would come pounding on Taft's door demanding the truth—something that couldn't be found in any of the answers he gave people.

Except my own team. They knew. Would the rumors reach them and let them know something very strange was happening?

Would they care if they did? I shouldn't have left as I had without a word. We had ways of communicating outside of OAC grids. I could've used them. But I'd been too wrapped up in figuring out what was happening between Magnus and I to give it a first thought. From my spot in the corner of Taft's office—he'd decided he didn't want me at his feet at all—I gauged again how long it would take me to reach his window versus how long it would take him. If I chewed off my leash, jumped through the window, landed two stories down, gathered my bearings, and used a shard of glass to somehow slice the collar from me, then maybe I could—come to my senses. Too many things could go wrong, including me stabbing myself while crashing through a window.

"I'll take you out in a moment," Taft said, his tone indulgent. He must've interpreted my staring at the window as needing to pee. "I figured you might need a walk to do your business soon. Though, with this, it will be a much shorter stroll." He pointed at his shin. He'd changed his pants, but I saw the thick bandage that made the fabric around his thigh tighter.

I wished I had rabies.

Taft stood, sauntering over to where I was tied up. He limped only slightly, but each dip felt like a victory. When he was close, he held out his hand over my head like he meant to pet me. I pulled back and growled.

Taft sighed. "I knew this was going to be rocky. But I did it anyway because it is the right thing. That's what a good alpha does, Wynn. Don't worry. You'll understand one day. You'll look at how even though you bit me I'm still willing to care for you and meet your needs. I'm not making you squat on a training pad like some others would. Like that fucking Gray would."

Taft didn't know the first thing about being an upstanding alpha. I was as much to blame as anyone for not seeing the true wolf behind Taft. No wonder he'd never shifted in front of anyone. He was probably a greasy, flea-ridden mess. He stared at me for a long second, annoyance flashing in his eyes before he tried to hide it. "You'll see, Wynn. Not today or tomorrow. But I'll get you home, you'll learn your place, and then you'll see how happy you can be."

Why had he even come to the OAC?

"I know you're angry now, but one day, you'll thank me for taking care of you."

A phone rang at his desk, but it wasn't the line on his desk that rang with official OAC business. This phone was in a drawer. He pulled it out and listened to whoever was on the other end. "Very good," he said after a few seconds. "Call me again when it is finished."

When it is finished? When what was finished? Magnus? Had that been the assassin he'd sent after me? So soon? The other agent couldn't have even glanced at Magnus's file before heading his way. Was he still in South Side or had he gone back to his penthouse? Who could I call to warn? Could I call the agent and explain the situation? Would they believe me?

I had a billion questions, no answers, and a fucking leash around my neck. I reared back, pulling tightly on my restraint.

"Shh, Wynn, you'll hurt yourself."

I barked at him loudly and repeatedly. Barks had different tones. Some were low and full of warning, others were excited, and this one was more of a yip. A ridiculous sound to make but also the most annoying. I yipped over and over, the same high pitched, nails-on-a-chalkboard shriek.

Eventually, Taft roared out his annoyance. "Shut up!" he bellowed.

I didn't obey. But I did keep pulling, knocking over the potted plant and sending dirt and debris across the carpet, slamming into the table and scattering the contents. I was making a mess of his office while Taft just looked at me like I was a child throwing a tantrum.

Then he stood, I braced for a strike, but he walked by me to the door. "Tear this place apart, Wynn. I don't care. Everything in here is funded by the OAC. Smash it to bits if it makes you feel better. I happen to love spending their money, and since it is clear you have to get this out of your system, I'll come back once you've calmed." He opened the door, locking it behind himself.

The moment he was gone, I tried scraping the collar off with my front paws, but it was fit too snugly around my throat, and I couldn't get it over my ears. I thought about trying to pry something in there and bending it off, but I could get stuck doing that just as easily as I could get myself free.

But I didn't really need to get the collar off. It wasn't as if Taft wouldn't know exactly where I was headed even if I did. I didn't even need to be in my human form. I just needed to save Magnus.

I made short work of the leash between my teeth, roaming freely around Taft's office. I tried to open the drawer that he'd put the phone in, but the drawer was locked. The other one was as well. On all fours, I tried pushing as much furniture as I could against the door but gave up quickly since the few chairs I'd managed to nudge over wouldn't provide me with much cover, and I needed to figure out how to get out, not how to stay in.

And after I saved Magnus, I needed to figure out how to expose Taft for what he was doing. To do that, I needed to figure out *what* Taft had been doing. I didn't want to even imagine the possibility that Taft had been using the

OAC to eliminate alphas who didn't expressly deserve it, but if it smelled like shit and looked like shit...

After pacing the space of his office—while trying to still sound like I was throwing a massive temper tantrum—I realized my first horrible plan had been my best option. There wasn't a vent large enough for me to crawl through—something that would've been made more difficult in my current form—and there was no way I was getting out by trotting down the hallway. But if I could jump from the window to the tree about fifteen feet away, I would be able to use that to get on the roof.

There wasn't time for a better plan. There might not even be time for this plan, but I couldn't let that thought take root. Magnus was still alive. He had to be.

Opening the window wasn't so difficult. I jumped up, bracing my front paws against the ledge to scope out my next step. A slab of cement waited for me two stories down if I failed. That wouldn't kill me, unless I was extraordinarily unlucky, but it would hurt, a lot. And the resulting broken bones would put me out of saving anyone for a long while. If any wolf on my team had come to me with a plan like this, I would've talked them out of it.

Was this why omegas were weak? Because we did stupid things for love? I'd never said the L-word to Magnus, and if I ever wanted a chance to, I needed to *jump out of a building* and pray I landed on the thick oak branch that extended my direction.

While in my wolf form.

I didn't have much time before Taft returned, but I felt like an idiot leaving empty-pawed. Circling Taft's desk, I checked the drawers—still locked—but there was a memory stick plugged into his computer. I didn't know if he used it as backup or if the thing was full of vacation pictures, but I yanked it out with my teeth before heading to the window.

I checked the ground outside. There weren't many out and about at this time of the day. Checking again wasn't going to make the distance any shorter, though, so I stepped back until my tail hit the wall opposite to the window, put my head down, and ran. I leapt into the air, sailing past the window ledge, over the spot on the branch I'd intended to land, and slammed into the trunk of the tree. I ducked my head away, hitting my shoulder instead. I'd see the aftermath of that on my shoulder the next day, but at least I didn't swallow the memory stick.

Without a look behind, I skittered down the branch hanging over the building awning. My next move was more of a fall than a jump, but I landed on the roof anyway, my claws scraping against the tiles. I had no way of knowing how the collar around my neck tracked my location, but since it did inhibit me from shifting—any time I tried it, I felt only a building pressure and then nothing—I could only assume Taft hadn't been lying about the other part. But, if he had the location tracker on his person, then he already knew I was no longer in his office. Which meant I needed to get out and fast.

Somewhere on the other side of the building, I hear an engine roar to life. I took off, blindly jumping off the roof while hoping it was the landscapers. I landed in a heap of leaves, sticks, and other grass clippings. The truck continued forward down the road, taking me away from Taft's office, slowing only a moment at the gate before hitting the highway.

I spit the memory stick onto my paw while I rode, blades of grass rising and swirling around me while the rest of me started to itch. But I wasn't about to complain. I could've blindly jumped into a slew of horrible things or missed the truck entirely. Instead, I checked to make sure we were traveling the right direction and then hunched low, avoiding the wind and staying out of sight until the truck turned into a parking lot. I jumped out without looking back to see if I'd been spotted. It didn't matter. Taft definitely knew I was gone by now, which meant he also knew where I was.

I checked the street signs, Magnus's work building was miles away, his apartment even farther than that. Shifting now meant finding someone to pay attention to me, miming what I needed from them, and then finding clothes so that people didn't call the cops on a naked omega running through the streets of downtown. I didn't get where I was by relying on other people to help me, and I couldn't start now. I put my head down and ran.

***

Magnus's building loomed ahead. No one bothered a collared omega running down the sidewalk. Most probably assumed I belonged to an alpha who had sent me on an errand while punishing me. I slipped through MattyCorp security to the elevator and used my paw to select the correct level while growling at anyone who tried to come in after me.

I spent the ride up imagining all the horrible sights that could be waiting for me. When the doors opened, I found the space nothing how I imagined it. Magnus's assistant's desk was empty—he still hadn't hired someone to replace Lloyd during his break. Thanks to his glass office walls, I could see Magnus sitting quietly behind his desk, staring at something on his screen while frowning.

Seeing him here, unharmed, sent a thrill of pure joy through me, followed by resentment. After everything I'd been through to escape and save him, being collared by the one alpha I was supposed to be able to trust, taking a blind leap of faith and running much of the way here, and I find Magnus at *work?*

I wasn't sure if he'd heard the door or sensed me staring because he looked up and our eyes locked. Mine still golden, but much lower to the floor. Magnus stood.

The elevator doors began to close, and I ran through.

"How are you… why are you…" Magnus couldn't seem to finish a question. His expression journeyed from relief to shock before settling on confusion. "Wynn, what is going on?"

I didn't think he meant about just right now either. He'd seen enough to know that I wasn't a prostitute like he imagined. I wasn't the meek but courageous omega, either. He deserved to know the truth, but first, I needed my collar off and to neutralize whoever was sent to finish what I couldn't.

I padded closer, stretching out my neck and whining.

"Is that his collar?" Magnus asked darkly. "It's lovely. Is that what you wanted to hear?" His voice sounded rough, like he was coming out of a cold. This close, I could see his dark circles, the red that rimmed his eyes.

I whined louder, lowering my head in deference to him while avoiding his eye contact.

"What is it, Wynn? Stop playing around. Shift and tell me with your words. Your meds must have worked fast if—"

We didn't have time for this. I didn't know who was coming or when. I barked, pushing my neck against his hand resting at his side. Magnus stumbled back, and I pushed forward.

"Wynn, what the hell? Just shift!"

I yipped.

Then Magnus grew very still. The hand I'd pressed my collared neck into began to shake. "You *can't* shift," he said, his voice monotone but full of anger.

His fingers grabbed for the buckle, jerking me around a little in his haste to get it off of me. The moment I was

147

free, I shifted. I was completely naked and a little cold after having fur for so long, but none of that mattered. "Taft isn't my alpha—he is my director. I'm an agent for a secret organization called the Omega Assassins Club and was sent to kill you, but then I discovered that what Taft said you'd done didn't line up with reality and I got confused and fell for you which made Taft angry and now I need to get you to a secure location before the replacement assassin he sent finishes the job."

Magnus's eyes filled with fire. "Your boss collared you? Forced you to stay in wolf form?"

"He said it was the only way I could keep my job. I was to remain by his side, staying at his home until he believed I was rehabilitated."

"He wanted to force you to live with him?" Magnus thundered.

And despite the fact that Taft was surely on his way, that the OAC would think I was a traitor, and that an assassin was likely going to show up any moment, I smiled. Magnus's first worry was still me.

"Why is any of this funny? I swear to god, Wynn, if this is some stunt—"

"You knew there was something different about me from the beginning," I said, slipping my arms through the suit jacket Magnus handed me. "That first time you saw me, I wasn't acting as a prostitute. I was a baby assassin on my first field mission. That's why I refused your help. I needed information from the old alpha."

"You weren't old enough to be doing something like that—"

"Not old enough, not strong enough, not brave enough. Omegas are invisible because of all of that. *I* am invisible until I want you to see me."

Behind me, the elevator dinged, indicating someone was coming up.

"Who are you expecting?" I asked, whirling around to face the elevator while pushing Magnus behind me.

He grunted and stepped to the side, unaccustomed to being the one being protected. "Just another applicant. His interview was hours ago, but I postponed it. Carl's is closed today, and I was in no shape earlier to—"

A decision that may have saved his life. "Do you have any weapons?"

Magnus's eyes bulged. "What?"

"Guns? Knives?"

"This is an office, Wynn. Why would I—"

The elevator car settled, dinging softly before the double doors opened and revealed the passenger.

The omega was dressed in a three-piece tweed suit. His brown hair was combed back and he wore glasses that I knew he didn't need. He looked dapper—for a fucking backstabbing piece of garbage.

"Nolan," I snarled, sinking low.

Nolan couldn't quite hide his initial shock. He hadn't expected to find me, pantsless, swimming in a suit jacket several sizes too big. But, when Magnus peeked out from behind me, Nolan's eyes narrowed with determination. Taft must've promised him something after the successful completion of this mission. Something worth fighting me for. He pulled a silver device out of his jacket, stuck it to the navigation panel on the elevator, and pressed a button. The doors shut behind him. Nolan's eyes studied me. "Nice look. A little dressed down for the workplace, but…"

I crouched low, preparing my body to move. "Stop, Nolan. I took the same class in witty pre-violence banter. Let's cut to the end where you don't do this."

"Do what?" Magnus asked. It was getting harder to keep his bulky frame behind me.

"Magnus, he's here to kill you," I hissed, wondering if he'd been paying attention at all.

"Like you were?" he asked, but with a sarcasm that implied he didn't quite believe me.

I almost didn't blame him. Out of every reason he'd probably come up with to explain my behaviors, assassin belonging to a secret club that helped the weak probably wasn't one of them. "Can you just—stay behind me?"

"Awww, that's cute," Nolan replied. He'd moved closer, but I'd been too distracted with Magnus to notice.

"You don't have to do this, Nolan. Whatever Taft is promising you—"

"Promising me?" Nolan asked, his lips twisting into a sneer. "I *asked* for this mission. That alpha needs to die. I don't even care what he was originally sentenced for. He should be killed for what he's done to *you*. You were one of the best agents I've ever met until this man made you turn on your home and family. I've told you all from the beginning—alphas are like tumors. The only effective way of handling them is to cut them from your life completely." He reached behind his body, revealing a large hunting knife that he held, poised for action.

I fell back behind the desk, pushing Magnus back while keeping my eyes on Nolan.

"He's not here to interview," Magnus said.

"He's a bright one," Nolan quipped.

I wished I could turn my face away to look at Magnus, if only for a second, but I didn't dare divert my attention. But, when we settled behind the desk, my eyes landed on Magnus's computer screen. He'd been looking at a page of search results for the query OAC with at least fifteen tabs opened to varying organizations with matching acronyms. *What the hell was the Ocelot Accounting Center?*

"You were looking for me?" I asked Magnus while staring at Nolan, who had inched even closer.

"Of course I was. Not trusting you was the biggest mistake I've made. I knew the moment that alpha came. I've been trying to find you the minute you left. I didn't have much to go on."

This was why it was important to remain emotionally detached during a mission. My body felt suddenly light. Butterflies collided in my stomach. I wanted to stop everything and kiss my alpha silly. And yet Nolan still held the same wickedly sharp knife.

"Enough of this, Wynn," Nolan said, crouching low.

My wolf paced in response, preparing for a fight.

"You had your fun. Kill him with me, we'll go back to the OAC, and—"

"That isn't happening, Nolan. It's two to one here. What sort of outcome are you expecting?"

Nolan gripped the knife, utter focus on his face. "We both know it's one on one. Is he worth this? Killing a member of your team? A packmate?"

Before I could answer, Nolan launched forward. The question had been a distraction, and while my stupid ass was sitting there pondering the answer, Nolan was nearly on top of me. He thrust for my gut. Magnus hollered, and I bent to the side, knocking Magnus back with my hip while avoiding the long blade.

Nolan didn't give me a chance to recover. He advanced, swiping with his knife. This time, the blade caught my bicep, slicing through the suit jacket like it didn't exist. I yelped while sweeping diagonally with my right leg and knocking Nolan back against the desk top.

I heard Magnus calling for security, but if I knew Nolan, the silver device he'd placed on the elevator was keeping help from reaching us, and the stairs would be equally obstructed. It's what I might have done had I expected trouble on a job.

"Magnus!" I deflected another attack from Nolan and then pushed the office chair toward him. It felt like we were back at the OAC, training while sparring at high speed. "They need to shut down the building. No one gets in." We didn't need Taft and reinforcements making their way up. Or catching us on our way out.

"Don't worry," Nolan said, pushing the chair out of the way. "Neither of you are walking out."

I snarled at Nolan's knife as it glinted in the sunlight. I would've given an inch of my dick for a weapon at that very moment. As I sunk low, ready to defend, I spotted a second glint. I reached for it, discovering a silver letter opener.

Did I say an inch?

I launched forward, striking fast before scrambling back. Nolan had to switch hands, holding his knife in his weaker grip as blood leaked from his shoulder. "I don't want to hurt you more, Nolan. Let us go. You can come too. I'll explain it all."

"Shut up, Wynn. You won't fool me like you did our team. Come with me. I'll explain how you've been brainwashed."

"I haven't been—" I bit my tongue. Arguing now would solve nothing.

Magnus appeared at my side, hands out toward Nolan like he was going to talk him down or something. I turned toward him a second too late, watching Nolan twist his body as he thrust forward. There wasn't time to counter, only deflect. I grabbed Magnus's elbow for leverage, twisting my body to face his while providing a buffer for the knife that Nolan slid into my back.

I waited for my body to react, for the blood to start pouring or my muscles to seize. I looked into the horror radiating from Magnus's face as he wrapped his arms around me and pulled us both away.

"Why would you do that?" Magnus and Nolan asked at the same time.

"Because I love you!" I said, pushing him behind me before stretching my shoulder out, wondering why I wasn't dead or dying. I turned to Nolan. "Because I love him."

Nolan still held the knife. Only the very tip was red. He'd pulled back at the last second, something not only difficult to do, but something he'd had no reason to do.

"Nolan," I said, my tone pleading. Earlier, I'd gone for the shoulder instead of the gut with the letter opener because I didn't want to hurt him severely. Nolan could've killed me just now.

Omega against omega. It didn't feel right.

Nolan's face softened in response a moment before there was a sharp pop. A hiss of static followed, and his eyes fluttered closed. I jerked forward as if to catch him, but he crumpled to the ground in a heap.

"Nolan?"

"He's not dead," Magnus said grimly. He held a small, black, rectangular object in his hand. "Long-distance stunner. Another thing I'd been working on in a line of omega self-defense items I've been developing."

I dropped to Nolan's side, rolling his body out straight so he wouldn't cut off his circulation.

"It delivers a single, concentrated blast up to ten feet away. But the biometrics don't always work, and the device itself is not one hundred percent reliable."

"It worked when we needed it to." I handed Magnus the hunting knife. "Please tell me you have a fancy billionaire way of getting out of this building?"

"There is the helicopter on the roof. It isn't a silent, practically undetectable tactical chopper—"

I pulled Nolan's pants from his body. He wore shorts underneath so I didn't think he would mind if I covered my bottom half. "If Taft isn't here, he will be soon." The collar was on the desktop, next to the memory stick. I grabbed the stick and pointed at the collar. "This is tracking our location. What should we—"

Magnus slammed his fist down on the desktop. The monitor wiggled, and the wood made a splintering sound. When he raised his hand, the tiny box on the collar that had housed the tracking device and shift inhibitor was cracked and in pieces. "Now it doesn't. Come on. The pilot is firing up the chopper."

CHAPTER FOURTEEN
Magnus

My security guard, Stu, had the helipad ready for when we landed on the roof of my penthouse ten minutes later. The entire flight, Wynn watched the perimeter for any sign of Taft. He looked different now than before he'd left. While I knew some of that had to do with his feelings over my betrayal of his trust, some of it was also just him allowing himself to be who he really was.

He sat straight, and while he wasn't necessarily still, his motions had a fluid grace, like water diverting around a series of stones, smooth, seamless and free. If I was to believe all the evidence in front of me, including Wynn's own confession, then I was with a trained killer. One that had been sent after me.

I thanked the pilot after we'd exited, sending him back to the airfield before directing Stu to perform an emergency evacuation with the story that a gas leak had been detected. He was to get everyone out, offering anyone who had no place to go a room in the hotel down the street. Stu nodded curtly at the end of my instructions and without a single question headed off to put the plan in action. We'd done exercises like this one in the past, preparing in case there was ever a real emergency, but he could tell this time was no training. "After you're sure they're all gone, you go home, Stu. I don't want you staying," I said.

Stu paused then. He turned back to me. "Sir, if you're in trouble—"

"No trouble," I replied cheerily. None I wanted to share, anyway. "Come in late tomorrow too." I looked to Wynn. "Or maybe take a paid day of vacation. I'll let you know." He'd be getting several weeks of vacation added to his employment package after all this.

Wynn stood a few feet away during the exchange, his right arm wrapped around his middle. I needed to get him in my penthouse so I could take a look at his back. I still wasn't sure how he wasn't dead. I'd seen the intent in the other omega's eyes. The moment I'd stepped to Wynn's side, I'd realized my mistake. At that time, I'd thought my repercussion was going to be death. Then Wynn had moved to my front, shielding my body with his.

"Wynn, come on. My penthouse is the safest place for us right now." I reached my hand toward him and waited for him to grab it, but what I wanted to do was scoop him into my arms and never let go.

He looked down at my hand, and for a second, I wasn't sure if he would accept it. He still only had my suit jacket with no shirt and Nolan's pants. His eyes had dark circles from exhaustion and stress, but he was here, with me, even after I'd been sure that would never happen again.

Since meeting him for the second time, I kept pushing him away, only to run back and accept him wholeheartedly. I was done pushing—that was, if he could accept me after what I'd done.

He let me bring him down to the penthouse where I disabled the elevator from reaching our floor while also locking the stairs. I activated the security screens on the windows and turned on the television, switching it to the mode that would allow me to view the feed from all the security cameras. There were several in the lobby and many outside, pointing both to the entrances and exits and at the street as well as cameras on every floor and space that wasn't private. People were busy packing the necessities and flowing out onto the street. At least they wouldn't be caught in any crossfires if Taft did bring the fight here as Wynn seemed to think he would.

"Let me take a look at your shoulder," I said as Wynn raced from room to room, confirming they were empty.

"It's fine," he said, brushing my worry away.

"Wynn, just let me look at it!" My tone was snappier than I should've allowed, but the stress of the moment was starting to weigh on me as well. Someone had tried to have me killed. Was trying.

Wynn stalked close. I kept my feet planted on my living room rug as he neared. "Or what? Will you call and tell on me again? Want Taft's direct line?" His words were teasing, but the hurt was still there.

"I'm sorry. I should've trusted you."

Wynn nodded, sliding my jacket off and hanging it over the back of the sofa. "I agree."

"He collared you."

Wynn scowled, and though it was quiet in the penthouse, his expression felt so loud. "Not with my consent."

Before I could stop them, mental images of Wynn, forced to strip, shift, and be collared filled my mind. When I imagined Taft on the other end of it all, my chest began to vibrate with growls. "I don't blame you for any of what happened to you, Wynn. It was my fault. I put the phone together. I wasn't able to wait for you to be ready to tell me." I could have said that alphas weren't great at waiting for information, but that was a bullshit excuse. I wasn't going to hide behind the stereotype of what I was when I knew I was so much more. "Did he do anything else?" I asked, not because I craved the gory details but because I wanted to be able to help Wynn moving forward as best as I could.

"He didn't have a chance to. If he catches us here, though—"

"He can't get in. Not unless he brings the building down, and to do that, he would need a lot of explosives."

That got Wynn moving around, checking the door, the windows, turning on the television to see if there was any news coverage. "We're sitting ducks up here," he murmured before his checking and re-checking dissolved into pacing from the living room to the door and back. "We need weapons."

"Okay, Wynn, hang on. *Stop.*" I stood in his way, hands up. "Just let me check your shoulder. Please. Then, after, we can strap us both up with all the kitchen knives in the drawers."

The corner of Wynn's lip tweaked in an almost smile. "You don't have any more prototypes? A supersonic alpha blaster or anything?"

"I don't keep my work at home for a reason." I gestured for him to sit. He was already shirtless so I could see the wound. It had been bleeding, but that looked like it had stopped. I went into the kitchen for a towel and the first aid kit.

"It's really fine," Wynn said when he saw me return with supplies.

"I know. Just let me clean it up for my own peace of mind." I used the saline to rinse the wound, wiping it clean before applying gauze and a bandage. "So, Nolan, he's one of your assassin co-workers?"

Wynn snorted. "He's on my team, on the OAC."

"And you… kill people?"

"Alphas," he replied without inflection.

My pulse raced, but at the same time, I wasn't afraid of the man in front of me.

That was a lie. I was afraid, but not of him hurting me physically.

Wynn turned and searched my face. "I knew you wouldn't understand," he said darkly before getting up and going into the master bedroom. I followed him to my closet where he chose a shirt.

I was pathetic enough to be pleased that he'd still be wearing my scent.

"Help me understand, Wynn. You kill people. My work is in direct opposition to that."

Wynn spun toward me, his eyes alight with anger. He took a step that turned into a stumble. I caught him, keeping hold until he had his balance.

"You're exhausted and I assume hungry. Taft isn't getting up here without a tank and an army. Let me make you something."

He pushed me back, but it didn't have any of the strength he normally had. "I'm fine—"

"No, you aren't. Stop saying that you're fine! You're wobbling on your feet. You've been through something traumatic—"

"Traumatic?" Wynn asked.

"Being collared—"

His laugh cut off the rest of my sentence. "That wasn't traumatic. Not compared to what I've seen."

"Look, you're a badass, okay? I had no doubt of that before I knew what you are and have no doubt of it now, but being collared against your will is still a shitty thing. Even if it isn't the shittiest thing. You should be allowed to have feelings about it." When he didn't immediately cut me off, I took a chance, grabbing his hand and bringing him back to the kitchen. He sat quietly while I pulled out the ingredients for a basic sandwich. "This Taft, did you know he was in love with you?"

Wynn jerked away from my words, nearly toppling back from his position perched on the stool on the other side of the counter. "Not love," he snarled.

"No, you're right. Did you know that he wanted to own you?" I slapped several layers of turkey onto a bed of pickles, hoping Wynn liked his sandwiches the same way I did. He looked so small and young on his stool. I reminded myself that he was around a decade my junior, which didn't mean he couldn't take care of himself, but it didn't stop me from wanting to take care of him either.

"I didn't realize until it was too late. I'd felt strange vibes from him, but I thought it was this mission, my stress, and confusion."

"The mission… you mean me?" I asked, setting his plate in front of him.

He smirked at the sandwich, cut into fours. "You were a troubling one from the beginning. That man you saw me with years ago, the alpha—"

"The one who disappeared?"

Wynn took a bite and looked away toward the shaded windows.

"He didn't disappear…"

"Well, he did, technically."

"Did you kill him?"

Wynn set the sandwich down and looked at me with his stubborn chin raised. "Would it matter if I had?"

"Wynn, you were ten. Yes, it would matter."

He sat straight and rigid on the stool. "It would matter because I was young or because I'd killed?"

"That feels like a trick question."

"It isn't. You either accept what I've done or you don't." He pushed the plate from him even though he'd only eaten a quarter.

I checked the security cameras running live on the TV. Most of the occupants were gone. The stream of people exiting the building was just a trickle. I didn't spot anyone who looked unusual, and while I knew that didn't mean they weren't there, they still weren't getting up here without me knowing.

"I shouldn't have come here." He stood. I was so scared he would try to walk right out that I moved to block his way. He didn't, though. He just stood there, wobbly and unbalanced.

"Wynn," I whispered, reaching for him. When his head hit my chest, it was like he dissolved. The iron straightness of his spine evaporated, and he sank into me.

He pressed his face into the spot above my heart as the first shuddering sob wrenched from him. "I have you," I assured him while rubbing his back. "I have you." And I did. Even though I still had a thousand questions, I knew the answers wouldn't change how I felt about the omega in my arms. Because no matter what he'd done, he *was* mine. Not in a dominating, possessive way, but in the way that meant he was mine to love, to protect.

"He made me feel powerless," Wynn murmured. "Taft, when he collared me, I felt trapped. He said it was temporary, but I knew by the way he lied to everyone that he had no intention of ever letting me go. Then, when he told me he'd sent another assassin, for a split second I gave up. I didn't see a way out. I didn't want one, not if you weren't alive."

"Don't ever say that, Wynn. Your life is worth living on its own, separate from me. Though I'm glad you won't have to try."

He sniffed and leaned back enough to look up into my face. "I still might. Taft will come. He's not just doing his job—he's angry. This is personal now. And he's got the might of the OAC behind him."

"Tell me more about the OAC now I know it doesn't stand for Ohio Artists Collective." The hours I'd spent trying to research with what little information I'd had had been frustrating to say the least.

He smirked and sat back down. This time, I sat beside him. I waited for him to start eating before I took my first bite. "You're about as good at spying as I am," he said with his mouth full.

"Was that what you were doing that night in my office?" I felt no anger thinking about that night now that I had a new perspective.

"I was supposed to find the schematics for your omega chip, deliver them to the client, and then…"

I made a motion with my finger across my neck. Wynn nodded.

Even if Wynn gave me three guesses to uncover who had hired him, I only needed one. "It was Visadore, wasn't it?"

"Yes. After I went AWOL, Taft said that Visadore didn't even want the schematics anymore. They just want you dead."

That took cutthroat business to a new level. "I can deal with that later."

Wynn jerked his head up. "How? And what do you mean, later? After we defeat the entire OAC?"

"Seems to me like we don't need to do that. Just Taft."

Wynn shook his head before I finished. "But Taft is operating under the orders from the founders—"

"Is he?" I asked, and Wynn fell silent. "What proof do you have of that, other than that he told you? He's proven his word means shit. He's proven he'll say and do anything to get what he wants. That reminds me—what did he say to you at the hotel, to make you leave? I was sure you were going to fight."

"Nolan had his laser sight trained on your forehead. Taft said, 'Come now or I'll have him killed.' If I hadn't gone, Nolan would've taken the shot."

I'd come so close to death, without ever realizing. "For a man sent to kill me, you sure did save my life a lot." And a man who did that wasn't a rudderless murderer. "Tell me about the OAC. All of it, from your first day to right this moment."

Wynn's face went a little pale. "It isn't a good story."

"I assumed as much," I said with a smile. I leaned over, kissing him softly on the forehead. "Just know there's nothing you can say that will change how I feel. Plus, you said I love you to me already, and there are no takesy backsies, so…"

He smiled and pushed me softly. His hand lingered on my shoulder, sliding down my arm to my hand where he squeezed. "It started when I was nine…"

***

Night had come without an appearance from Taft. I sat in a chair near to the bed where Wynn was sleeping, but in a position that allowed me to monitor the security feeds without losing sight of him. I'd sent Stu home since I didn't want him getting caught up in anything, leaving me and Wynn alone in the building—for now.

Wynn had done exactly as I'd asked, telling me every rage-inducing moment that brought him to the OAC and all that occurred after before falling asleep the moment his head hit the pillow.

From what he'd told me, the OAC was an organization with a clear goal: eliminating the worst of the alphas in the world. My own personal feelings aside, I could get behind their mission statement. But the way Wynn described it made it seem like a system lacking in checks and balances, which made it ripe for corrupting. And now Taft had.

Before he'd fallen asleep, Wynn had revealed the memory stick he'd taken from Taft's computer. He'd given it to me, promising he would just close his eyes for twenty minutes. That had been two hours ago.

I wanted Wynn to sleep, but I also needed answers, so I grabbed my laptop, removed it from the network, and then used it to scan the memory stick for a tracker—I'd already made that mistake once. I expected the information to be encrypted, and it was. I was also lucky to have developed a business around cybersecurity.

I booted the decryption program and set the laptop on the ground while I waited. The speed of the program depended on the strength of the security. A simple password would've taken seconds. I assumed this would take at least an hour, so when the program alerted me thirty minutes later, I was surprised.

The information within didn't look like vacation photos, so that was one theory debunked. There were files. Dossiers of men—all alphas. And there were images, grainy black-and-white photos of men who did not know their picture was being taken. When I scrolled to the end, I found my own picture, taken right outside the entrance to MattyCorp.

"Is that from Taft's computer?" Wynn asked, his voice thick with sleep. He'd rolled over, taking the blanket with him while hugging the bottom half of the pillow under his head.

"Yes, and don't worry, I'm off the network. No way of tracking me from here." As if that mattered now. "Do any of these alphas look familiar? Other than myself, of course."

Wynn's eyes darted left to right over the screen as I opened each image file. "None of them were targets of mine. So that's what's on there, our next missions? Hold on, go back."

I scrolled back to a page of stats. Some of them made sense, like height and weight. Others didn't, but the dollar sign in the corner was unmistakable. "That's a lot of zeros," I said, letting out a low whistle.

"That's too many zeros. Part of the OAC's mission is helping the weak and the poor. We don't get paid numbers like this because our clients aren't supposed to have this kind of money. It's why we rely so much on the founders and investors."

"But if one or two of these cases are slipped in among the valid ones, the agent completes the mission as needed, Taft is paid, and no one is the wiser, then it looks like he's found himself a goldmine."

"He's *using* us," Wynn said, his voice vibrating with anger. "You were right all along. I'm not much more than a prostitute."

"Hey, don't say that. You didn't know. And his first mistake was sending you, right? I think maybe his infatuation with you clouded his judgment of who you are as a person. But who you are is thoughtful, caring, inquisitive. I'm alive because you asked questions."

I set the laptop down and climbed into bed instead. My omega needed my comfort more in that moment. "I'll— *we'll* fix this, Wynn. What about your team? Are any of them loyal enough to you that they'd let you explain the situation?"

"I think so? River, Van, and Zed are my pack brothers. But, up until a few days ago, I would've said you could trust Taft as well."

"What about the founders?"

"I wouldn't even know how to contact them. Only Taft had that connection—" He sat up abruptly, pulling from my grasp with a curse. "We really were just docile idiots, ripe for the taking when Taft waltzed in."

"That isn't fair. You had no part in his hiring. Of
course you assumed the man placed in a position of power
by those already in power was going to be trustworthy.
And from the looks of this, he did his job correctly until
now."

"*If* this is the first case," Wynn added darkly.

"True, but I have a hunch it is. We'll have to interview
every agent and compare the mission they were sent on
with the records on file."

Wynn gave me a half-smile. "Are you in the OAC
now?"

"Well, my omega is, so I thought I'd tag along." I shot
him a covert look.

He smiled, and his cheeks were tinted pink. The food
and rest had done a lot for his complexion. The bags
under his eyes were still there, but not quite as
pronounced.

"Your omega," he repeated. Then, his eyes filled with
tears. "I don't know how you still want me. I can't stop
pulling apart every mission I went on under Taft's
leadership. So many men begged, told me I had the wrong
guy, and I was *so sure* I didn't. That I was the one doing the
right thing for people who couldn't protect themselves.
But what if I wasn't?" His question came out barely louder
than a whisper.

"Then we'll deal with that too, mate. We'll handle it all,
together." I wiped away his tears but let him remain with
his head slumped.

"Call me mate again," he murmured quietly. "Please.
Even though I don't deserve it. Even though you deserve
better. Even though—"

I kissed him softly on the nose. "Mate. You are my
mate. This time, I'm saying it for good. I want to go to the
courthouse and make it official. Is there anyone in your life
I need to ask?"

"Like, for permission?" Wynn asked, his eyebrows furrowed in confusion. "Before, I would've said Taft, but..."

"I'm not asking him," I said with a growl.

Wynn smiled. "I don't think he would say yes anyway."

That reminded me of the way Taft had been around Wynn. The way he'd spoken of Wynn. The way he'd assumed ownership of him. My blood boiled as my wolf ached for me to reestablish my claim. *Not the right time, buddy*, I tried to tell him, but that didn't stop the blood from rushing between my legs.

Ignoring my erection became more difficult the moment I felt Wynn's fingers around my length. "Wynn, you don't have to—"

"I know," he replied. In the next minute, I was on my back, and he was on top of me. "I *want* to. With you, I always want to."

He bent his head slowly, like he was giving me a chance to put a stop to it. Instead, I gripped the hair at the back of his head, holding him in place for my lips. For a few moments, there was a battle of wills. Both wanted the upper hand. Both wanted to control the kiss. I growled, caught up in the moment. The sound made him whimper, and as he did, he became pliant, obedient in my grasp. "I love when you give up to me. Because I know every time it's what you're choosing. I can't make you do anything, omega."

His eyes flashed with desire. "Anything," he repeated, licking his lips.

"Just having you here," I told him while working my shirt off of his frame. "When I thought I'd never see you again..."

Luckily for me, he'd taken the pants off before his nap. I yanked down the seam of his underwear, ripping it free.

"Not trusting you was the worst mistake I ever made. I'll never forgive myself for handing you over."

Wynn pressed his lips on mine hard. "You're forgiven—"

"No, you can't let me off that easily—"

He pressed his index finger against my lips. "You're forgiven if you claim me now. My life—it's full of violence and hatred. Show me love."

I brought our mouths together, slowing down my kisses. My tongue glided lazily along the line of his teeth, flicking against his tongue before I pulled back, continuing my kisses over his ear and down his neck. I licked down his collarbone, exploring his body as if we hadn't a care in the world. His skin shook and trembled under my lips, but I kept him on top, straddling me. Though it seemed as if the position put him in power, he was like a boat, and I was the rudder guiding us through passion-filled waters.

"This is the only thing that feels right to me," Wynn murmured. "Being with you, touching you, feeling you. I couldn't do anything to make that stop happening."

I reached blindly to my nightstand. "Then don't," I said, pressing my lube-slicked fingers into his tight pucker. He moaned and clenched down, drawing each digit deeper with his muscles. "Stay with me forever, mate." He groaned as I penetrated him slowly with my fingers. My thrusts were as deliberate as they were deep. I scissored my fingers inside of him, listening to his moans and pulling his face toward mine so I could taste them as well.

His skin grew slick with sweat, and his body began to tremble as I used everything I'd learned to lead him to the edge of orgasm, only so I could dance away from it and draw him back. He never complained, but started making short, mewling noises of longing. His body trembled with desire, and though he was on top, I held him up.

"What does my omega want?" I asked, our foreheads pressed together.

"You," Wynn replied. "I don't want it. I need it. Please, give me your alpha dick." This sentiment coming from anyone else's lips would've made my eyes roll. From Wynn, it made my cock jerk, and my muscles clench.

I pulled my hand free, using the excess lube on my shaft before lifting Wynn so he was poised with his hole pressing on my tip. He tried to push himself down and claim my cock, but I held him tightly. Finally, he gave up, slumping in my grip. I lowered him slowly, allowing his body to adjust but unrelenting in my quest to bury my entire length inside of him. He moaned and wailed, throwing his head side to side as I fed him inch by inch.

When he was fully seated, I held him for a long moment, content to feel his warmth and the tight pressure of his canal flexing over and massaging my shaft. He made soft noises but was otherwise content where he was, his face resting on my shoulder as I held him.

With my hands at his hips, I began to move, lifting his body up, all the way off, before beginning another slow descent.

"Oh my God, that feels… it's… Magnus!" he cried out as I bottomed out once more, pressing deep inside of him.

My movements hardly quickened as I continued to fuck him with excruciatingly slow, deliberate strokes. So much of our lives together had felt rushed. Even this moment was one we'd stolen, but I wasn't going to let my omega feel like he was anything less than the precious treasure that he was.

My strokes did eventually quicken, spurred on by my inner wolf who was only concerned with spilling seed. He wanted Wynn stuffed with my essence, scenting him from the inside out. I lifted Wynn again and slammed him back down, causing his head to fall back, face to the sky as he howled and his cock erupted. My hips thrust upward as the animal in me took over, pounding into him with none of my earlier gentleness.

Wynn still moaned just as loudly. His cock was already hard again, and as the onslaught continued, he clung to me, allowing me to do what I wanted with his body. But not because it was something I expected from him as an omega—because he *wanted* it. "Yes, yes, yes," he chanted in time with each upward thrust.

I stopped suddenly, bringing it all to a screeching halt while still buried inside his tight canal. "Tell me you're my omega," I said, hating that I needed to hear it, but needing to hear it all the same.

Wynn replied without a moment's hesitation. "I'm yours."

"And you'll be my mate?" I asked, punctuating the question with a quick pump of my hips.

"Yes!" he wailed.

"You'll live with me, by my side?" Another quick pump, in, then out.

"Fuck! Yes, Magnus, by your side."

"And you'll have my babies?" This time, I didn't stop at one thrust.

His voice shook, but he answered, "Yes!"

His reply was the only catalyst I needed. My balls drew tight as the tingling started, first at the base of my spine and then up and out, cascading down my shaft as I spilled all I had into him. "Mine!" I roared before latching down, covering his fading mating mark.

It would never fade again.

Before I could even pull back and wipe the sweat from his forehead, an alarm sounded in the front room. I lifted him from me, both of us wiping ourselves clean and dressing quickly.

"Does that mean there is someone in the building?" Wynn asked.

"It means a sensor was tripped." We stood in front of the television, still set to play the live feeds from the cameras stationed around the building. The lobby was still empty. The hallways were clear. I frowned.

"Where all do you have sensors?" Wynn asked.

I went to the console, tapping the screen so it would show me which alarm had been tripped. "This makes no sense. It's an outside sensor, one I put on the outer ledge because I was worried that pigeons were nesting inside the walls there."

"Can you show me on the cameras?" Wynn asked.

"No, there isn't one that catches that angle. Because it's there." I pointed to the corner of the penthouse where the ceiling in the living room met the wall of my office. "There's no access from the outside."

For some reason, Wynn smiled. "Not if you're a regular person. But if you're fucking Nolan. God, I hope he's seen the error of his ways," Wynn said, surging toward the doors to the balcony.

"Wait, wait, you're saying that Nolan climbed up this skyscraper—"

"No, that's ridiculous." Wynn unlocked the patio doors. "I'm saying he paraglided in and then rappelled from the roof."

CHAPTER FIFTEEN
Wynn

I knew it was more likely that Nolan was here to finish what he'd started rather than help us, but my gut told me he could've killed me in Magnus's office and didn't. Why bother with any of this if he wasn't also having doubts?

Except, now that I was out on the balcony, wind whipping my hair around as I peered up to the corner where Magnus had indicated there was a sensor, I felt a smidge foolish. "Nolan?" The balcony ended at least ten feet away and half a floor below the corner Magnus had pointed out.

Magnus was at my side, shaking with adrenaline. He didn't want us to be out here. I was beginning to doubt my own sanity. Every agent at the OAC had been trained to be able to crawl out of and into a variety of spaces. Nolan was one of the only omegas I knew who also had the strength to withstand the winds this high up, but Taft could've brought someone from any of the teams.

Except the moment I saw a figure slide out of the darkness like a spider on roller skates, I knew it was Nolan. We might not have gotten real close, but we'd trained together long enough for me to know how his body moved. "That was idiotic. How did you know it was me?" Nolan asked, landing in front of me.

"Because I knew you knew where I was. Are you here for Taft?" I asked.

"Would I be here talking if I was? More importantly, would I tell you? You see, this is why we should stay as far from alphas as possible. Sooner or later, one is going to tickle your nethers in a way that makes you feel special, and then it's like years of training never happened."

"Well, I could still just throw you from the balcony, so tell me why you're here, Nolan." I smiled because I was pretty sure I wouldn't throw him off the balcony, but also because a part of me thought I might.

"Because the OAC means more to me than anything. I thought you were responsible for fucking with it. But now I'm positive that isn't the case. It's Taft. I think he's—"

"Slipping in non-sanctioned missions for alphas that don't actually deserve it?"

Nolan frowned, likely because I'd stolen his big moment. "Yeah, but did you know that each of those missions also—"

"Comes with a fee that would make Taft a millionaire?"

Nolan snarled. "Fuck, you're annoying. Yes, to that as well. I did some digging. Your loverboy here had a hit put out on him by Visadore, a competing business. I think he thought you'd go in, realize you sucked at gathering information, and kill him out of frustration."

He held me in such high esteem.

"But why are you here now? Does he know?"

"He's going to attack the building at dawn," Nolan said. "He hasn't asked me or any of the other teams to prepare, but that's because he has to be careful."

"And you're telling us that now?" Magnus snapped. "I'll call the police—"

Nolan rounded on him. "And get more people killed?" He turned to me. "You can't like him for his brains."

"I invented the device that brought you to your ass this afternoon," Magnus quipped.

I smiled and then stepped between them, just in case.

"Thanks for that, by the way. Did you not see how I could have totally stabbed your sweet omega but decided not to? What does he do to thank me? I woke up with no pants."

I rubbed the back of my neck. "Sorry, that was me. So Taft's coming at dawn. I assume you have a plan?"

Nolan shrugged.

"A shrug isn't a plan," I said.

He threw his hands into the air. "Why do you expect me to come up with everything? I'm finding this all out as I go along. Like how he never told the founders shit. They never told him to collar you. They don't even know you were missing. No one but our team knows. Taft told us that if we talked about it, it would just make things worse for you. That fucking dick has so many lies spinning. They're about to all come crashing down around him. And I want to be there when it happens." He stopped talking and stared out at the city. When he spoke again, he sounded less like the cocky self-assured omega I was used to. "The OAC is my home, Wynn. I know you all whisper about me and think I'm a prick. I am one. And the rumors are all true, I volunteered for the OAC, begged to be let in, but that just means I'll defend it. And what Taft is doing with the OAC is the beginning of the end for us. Not unless we stop him."

Any lingering doubts I had about Nolan disappeared. There hadn't been a whiff of fabrication in his words. Only fervor. "But you don't have any idea of how?"

"Well, I do have one plan," Nolan said. "But you aren't going to like it."

***

"I hate it," Magnus said for the hundredth time since Nolan unveiled his idea. Nolan had left an hour earlier, saying he needed to get back to headquarters before anyone noticed he was missing.

That left Magnus uninterrupted in his attempts to talk me out of what we had planned for the next morning.

"I know you hate it, but do you have a better option?" I asked his back since he was turned away from me.

I watched his back muscles flex as he crossed his arms. "I won't do it. What you're asking of me... I can't even begin to—"

I approached him slowly. Not because I was afraid, but because I wasn't sure of what to say and wanted the extra time. "I can do it, Magnus. You don't have to."

"That's worse!" he hollered, spinning around only to come to an abrupt stop when I was right in front of him. He grabbed me, hugging me tightly. "How can you ask me to put you in danger?"

"If everything goes the way Nolan thinks it might, then there shouldn't be any danger, not the real kind."

"Are you listening to yourself? If *the man who you stabbed with a letter opener twelve hours ago* is correct? How do you know you can trust him?"

"Because of what he said about the OAC. It is his home. It gave him a new chance at life. That's what it did for us all, and in turn, we do that for other people. He loves it. Even if he is a little zealous when it comes to his ideas about alphas."

Magnus didn't reply, but he didn't argue either, which was an improvement. I took advantage of the short reprieve and went to the bathroom, splashing water on my face before turning to the toilet. I did my business and zipped before washing at the sink. Behind me, the toilet began to chime.

175

"Magnus?" I called out loud enough to be heard from the bathroom to the living room.

"What? What is it? Did something happen?" Magnus rushed in, his claws extended.

"Whoa, no, nothing is wrong. Except I broke your toilet."

Magnus made a face that was half-wince, half-grin.

"Not like that," I snapped. "There was a chime, and look, there's some kind of code."

"That's just your health report. The toilet is one of my own inventions. It's designed to evaluate your urine and provide a comprehensive health analysis. I thought it could help omegas with irregular heats track them a little better."

I peered over the screen, impressed at my mate's ingenuity while also offended that a toilet was trying to tell me to eat more greens. "What does checkpreg mean?"

He scratched his chin. "Checkpreg? No see, there is a space. Check preg. It means the user should take a pregnancy test because it detected trace amounts of hCG in the urine and—" Magnus spun around, lifting me in the air with a whoop before setting me down gently. "You're pregnant, Wynn. It's telling you you're pregnant."

"The toilet is telling me I'm pregnant," I repeated. "And you believe it? A talking toilet?"

"It isn't a talking—" He let out a noise of exasperation. "I can show you the science behind the diagnostics. It is sensitive but sound. Been telling me to cut back on my iron intake for weeks."

"So why haven't you?"

Magus shrugged. "I'm not gonna let a toilet tell me what to do."

A moment of silence passed between us.

"My heat was days ago," I said.

"Yeah, and it didn't last days longer like it should have, only hours."

"I thought that was because I had an alpha there to satisfy it."

Magnus puffed up proudly. I couldn't help but smile. "You *did* have an alpha there to satisfy you." He put his hand on my stomach, but the move felt too real, and I skittered away.

"If I am, it is very early. Too early for any other test to detect anything."

Magnus nodded. "That was part of the reason I didn't move forward with mass production. The system was still a little sensitive, diagnosing based off of one sample. Not so bad for you or me, but with someone already anxious, it was a recipe for disaster."

"Which is why we will ignore what the toilet said and continue with Nolan's plan."

Magnus shook his head. "No way in hell we're doing that plan now. I'll tell you what we're doing. We're calling the cops—"

"And telling them your assassin omega needs protecting from his mean boss? They'll have me in cuffs before you can finish explaining."

Magnus snapped his mouth closed, only to stick his finger in the air as another idea struck. "Then I'll call the guys. They can get here from South Side in a few hours and they'll—"

"Get their asses kicked or worse trying to infiltrate the OAC." I cupped his face, rubbing his jaw with my thumb. "I know you're just trying to help me, but you need to trust that I know what I'm doing now. It isn't like how it was before. Nolan is there in case anything happens."

"But I won't be." The words seemed ripped from his throat, tortured and raw. "I should be there. I'm your alpha."

I brought my other hand up, cupping his face tenderly. "You are. Which is crazy if you think about it. I have no business finding my mate, a guy like me? But I did, and somehow, you want me back, and now I could have this *life*." My voice cracked, forcing me to swallow several times before speaking. "But we'll have *nothing* if Taft isn't stopped. All of those pictures, all those men on that memory stick, they'll be tombstones. And even if the omegas responsible are somehow snagged by the regular authorities, Taft will still never see a single charge. And we'll never be able to rest." I kissed him and tried to not make it seem like the last kiss we'd ever share. "You can do this, Magnus. We can."

There was lightning in his gaze that quickly culminated into a full force, level five storm. I hated putting him in this position, knowing it would go against his very nature, but I couldn't hide and do nothing. Even if Taft never took on another unsanctioned hit, he'd still collared me against my will. He'd do it again to another omega if no one stopped him and *made* him see that omegas didn't exist for his pleasure. And, apparently, he was a very slow learner.

"I love you, Wynn," Magnus said with a mischievous smile. "Which is why you can't be upset that I wasn't *completely* honest with you about what I keep at home."

***

"It's seven. Nolan said that was the time." I watched Magnus pace from the security desk in the lobby, to the elevators and back.

"He could not show," Magus said.

"He'll show."

Magnus walked behind the desk, out of view to anyone outside and nearer enough for him to pull me close. "We could go," he said wistfully.

I didn't respond, partly because I didn't think he was expecting one and partly because I saw movement on the security cameras. A dark Land Rover pulled slowly into frame. "He's here."

Magnus stiffened. His face was tense, his jaw clenched.

I stood squarely in front of him. "Hit me."

He shook his head. "No, I can't."

Any other time in the world I would be over the moon to have found an alpha so respecting and gentle, but right now, I needed to look like I'd been through something harrowing. "Magnus! Hit me!"

"No!" Magnus roared, towering over me, his whole body tensed and ready for action.

"Fine." I spun around. Before he could grab my shirt at the back and stop me, I slammed my forehead against the corner of the wall. Pain exploded out from the spot, and my stomach rolled, but I inhaled slowly in my nose and out my mouth until the nausea passed.

"Wynn." Magnus sounded broken as he reached for me, but we didn't have time.

I took off around the desk, wobbly sprinting toward the double doors where I pushed through them and out onto the street—nearly getting hit by the Land Rover in the process.

Taft skidded to a stop. His eyes widened in surprise before narrowing. "I did it!" I gasped, groping at the driver's side door. "I killed him, Taft. I did it!"

Taft watched me for a long moment without ever rolling down his window. Then he pressed the button, bringing it down a crack. "Why the sudden change?" he asked.

"I just needed more time to see how right you were," I said, the words tasting bitter but necessary—like medicine. "Then, last night, he tried to force himself on me. You were right about him, Taft. It was a struggle," I gestured up to my bleeding head wound, "but I did it."

Again, Taft watched me. He raised a single eyebrow. "You're saying I should send in a cleanup crew? That you're ready to come home? Just like that?"

I swallowed the lump in my throat. "Yes."

Finally, Taft opened his door. He stepped out cautiously, his hands out and ready to react. "You're ready to come to my home?"

My wolf howled. I *was* home. "Yes, take me. Show me where I belong, Taft."

He reached for me, and I fell into him, letting my body press against his like a glove over a hand. My skin itched at the contact with another alpha that wasn't my own. My body had chosen Magnus and would not accept another— but I couldn't let Taft know that.

"Where's Nolan?" I asked, trying to sound casual.

Taft held me back, staring into my face. "Why did you assume he'd be with me?"

"I… uh…"

Taft ignored me and grabbed the handle of the knife at my waist, pulled it free and threw it over the Land Rover where it skittered somewhere on the sidewalk. "You'll understand if I'm a little jumpy," he said in reply to my questioning stare.

I tried to look guilty, dropping my eyes down to look at the center of his chest. "I understand. I broke your trust. I'll have to earn it back."

Taft nodded. He'd led us to the passenger side, where he opened the door and reached for something in the glove box. "Trust. It's interesting that you would bring that up since I no longer have any in you." He fit zip-tie handcuffs over my wrists and pulled until the plastic dug into my skin.

"Ouch!"

"Oh, I'm sorry, too tight?" he asked, his tone mocking and hard. "Did you think I would believe this?"

He shoved me into the passenger seat, smacking me across the face before reaching for the seatbelt and buckling me in. "You are a horrible liar, Wynn. And you must think me an old fool to fall for a plan so comical. What were you going to do, slink back into my good graces until you could find some evidence against me?" There was a moment of silence before he continued. "Or maybe you were hoping to use Nolan as a distraction? Is that why you asked if he was coming?"

He stomped around the car, sliding quickly into the driver's side. He fastened his buckle and then without warning slammed the side of his fist against my nose. I heard a crunch and felt warm blood beginning to pour freely. My head lolled to the side, away from him and toward the building where I saw Magnus burst through the double doors, screaming my name. He must have seen everything happening on the security camera.

Taft spotted him next and chuckled before slamming down on the gas. "Divine resurrection?" he taunted.

My head spun too quickly for me to do more than groan in response. Taft already had us to the other end of the block, where he blew right through a red light. At the early hour, there weren't many people out, but there were still a few honks.

Taft slammed his fists into the steering wheel while letting out a guttural roar. "I can't believe you thought that would work. It's offensive how incapable you think I am." His hand whipped out, and he grabbed a large chunk of my hair, yanking my head over the center console. "I'm an *alpha*, Wynn. I'm older than you, smarter than you, and stronger than you."

"You—" I licked my lips. "You won't get away with this. The OAC will find out."

"From who? You? You're going to live in my basement where you'll learn the proper way to serve your alpha. And the rest of your team is going to meet their untimely yet unavoidable deaths in the coming days. Nothing against them—they just know too much."

I made a noise between a cry and a gasp. My head pounded, and my fingers were beginning to tingle from how tight the cuffs were. I could only imagine what Magnus was going through.

Behind us, I heard sirens and tried to turn around to see if they were close, but the motion made me dizzy.

"Fuck! Did you call them?" Taft bellowed.

I rested my head back but turned to look at him. "With what?" I mumbled.

Taft yanked my jacket to the side, checking my pockets as he drove.

"I don't have anything." It was too hard to speak loudly so I whispered while halfheartedly trying to shove him away. "You blew through that red light."

Taft cursed, but at least he stopped trying to get into my pockets. He jabbed a few buttons on his console and then grabbed his gun, setting the barrel directly against my forehead. "Don't say a fucking word." Through the car speakers, I heard ringing and then the familiar timbre of Remington's voice.

"Speaking," Remington said.

"It's Taft. I went to look for *your* missing agent, and now I have some heat on my tail. Can you get rid of it?"

I longed to scream into the speakers that I was there, that Taft was evil, that he didn't give a shit about omegas and was using us for his own gain, but Taft never moved the gun.

There was some clicking on Remington's end, muffled static, and then, "I sent in a call near your location. All cars should be rerouted."

"Very well," Taft replied, his thumb edging toward the button that would disconnect the call.

"Sir, if I may ask, I've been hearing some odd whispers about Wynn. That's he's gone rogue. Sir, I've known Wynn since before his first day at OAC. He's dedicated to our cause. If something is going on with him, it would bear looking into. He wouldn't act without reason."

Taft's face went red. "Noted. Perhaps we will do an investigation, starting with how his handler had one job—to know where his agent was at all times—and how he could've possibly failed so miserably." Taft hung up after that, not giving Remington a chance to respond. Just like a coward. "I guess he'll need to meet his untimely end as well."

"So that's your plan? Kill everyone who finds out about you?"

The light ahead was red. This time, Taft slowed to a stop at the white line. He tapped his fingers against the steering wheel as he waited. "Kill or control, how an alpha should behave. Your team, your handler, your *alpha*—"

I gasped.

"That's right. Hope you said goodbye. And this time, the man sent to kill him won't fall in love with him instead. No more sending omegas to try to do an alpha's work."

"You're a monster."

The light turned green, and the car rolled forward. We were nearly out of the downtown district. From here, the roads would turn into highways.

"No, Wynn, the monster is you. I'm just a smart man who recognized a great opportunity. Omega Assassins Club," he spat. "Stupidest fucking thing I've ever heard. But I knew there was an untapped opportunity there. So I took the job, pretended to give a shit—every year I should've taken home the Oscar for best performance. It can't last forever. The rest of the omegas will catch on sooner or later, but why do I give a fuck? I have enough evidence to put each of you away. I'll leak it and then hop on my private jet heading to the Bahamas with pockets weighed with money and far less competition when the smoke clears and I make it back. If you're good, I might even let you join me. At my feet, of course."

The dash chimed, indicating an incoming call. Taft pressed his gun to my head again before answering. "What is it?" he barked.

"Sir, I've just heard some chatter on the police radio waves. Most cars were diverted, but one is still on your tail. I see your location on my map and recommend you take the next left. There's an alley there that will allow you to wait out of sight of the traffic surveillance cameras while they pass."

Taft smiled, entirely pleased with himself. "Thank you, Remington," he said as he took the turn, driving down a narrow road with tall buildings on either side.

"No problem, sir," Remington replied. "And one more thing. Nolan, you're in position."

Taft's face wrinkled with confusion. "What—?"

From the very backseat came a set of blurs, previously cloaked in fabric the exact shade and type of the car's interior. Nolan burst forward, immediately slamming his fists into Taft's face. Van slunk out of the back seat and to my door, where he opened it and sliced my belt free.

"Your face looks awful," Van said, thrusting his wrists toward me so I could tighten the zip tie binding his hands.

"You look amazing," I told him. Inside, Taft had regained some of his bearings. He reached for his gun.

"Where's Zed and River?" I asked.

A small body popped up from the roof and pushed back the tight black hood over his head, setting loose a mess of blond curls. "I hate being top," he whined before rolling over the roof toward the driver's side. He smashed a metal bar he retrieved from his sleeve against the window, shattering it before he tossed a canister inside. "Clear!" he shouted.

Nolan launched out the same door Van left open the moment before the canister went off, filling the inside with smoke.

Zed landed firmly at my side, coming from somewhere above. "They're on their way. Assume position," he said. River peeled off the tight black suit that had kept him concealed, throwing it into a pile of trash before helping Nolan and Zed with their zip ties and slipping on his own. He tightened the loops with his teeth.

Taft roared, but he'd managed to get his belt free and opened his door. He stomped around the car, heading to the five of us, pausing for only a moment when he saw us on our knees in the alley, our hands bound as we faced him.

Shaking in his rage, he raised his gun the exact moment blue and red colored lights lit up the alley.

"Drop the weapon!" a firm voice shouted among the sounds of tires coming to a sudden stop and heavy boots hitting the pavement. I didn't dare turn around, but I could hear us being surrounded.

"Drop your weapon, or we will be forced to fire!" another voice ordered.

"Please, help us!" River wailed, sounding every inch the terrified omega.

"He's kidnapped us!" Nolan added, raising his cuffed hands into the air while doing his own best impersonation of someone who was helpless.

Taft growled, his gun still pointed our way as realization dawned. "You planned this," he spat at me.

"Not my plan," I replied loud enough so the cops rushing in behind us couldn't hear. From the corner of my eye, I saw Nolan wink.

Taft looked from us to the cops rushing in. He tightened his grip on the handle but bent over at the last second, setting the gun on the ground and raising his hands over his head as the cops instructed.

They rushed in, three holding on to Taft as they cuffed him and searched for weapons.

"You don't understand," Taft said. "They are trained killers. They're attacking me."

The cops paused, looking at the line of us on our knees. Van was actively crying while Zed, River, and Nolan whimpered. My face throbbed, but the blood and bruises did a good job covering my inability to cry on cue.

"Yeah, really looks like they were giving you a run for your money, buddy. How long you been working that one over?" a cop asked, gesturing toward me.

"He did that to himself," Taft said. While he wasn't all wrong, the cop just scoffed when he saw the blood on Taft's hand from when he hit me after.

"Uh-huh. Put him in the back. I'll get these five loaded," the cop said to two other uniformed officers who led Taft toward a police cruiser. It was sad that it had taken the perfect setup for us to be sure the cops would take immediate action, but we'd ensured the scene they'd stumbled into had looked nothing short of sinister.

"I'm going to help you to your seats, and then the van will take you to the station where they'll do an exam while collecting your things for evidence," he explained, gently lifting Van from his knees to his feet. "I don't want to contaminate the evidence so they'll have to cut the ties free at the station. But don't worry. I'll get you seated and buckled."

One by one, he helped us to our feet and into a black van with the initials WPPD on the side. The back had an open layout with two benches on either side of the van that faced each other. A metal grate separated us from the driver, who gave us a short wave without turning. A second, silent figure in the passenger seat didn't acknowledge our presence.

"Thank you, sir. Thank you," River said as he climbed in, shakily landing on the smooth bench. He was the last of us, and after helping him buckle, the cop reached to shut the door—not before sending River a shy, but genuine smile.

"Just glad we got here in time," the cop said before shutting the door and tapping the back of the van twice.

The driver started the engine and pulled slowly away from the mayhem as the five of us just stared at each other. The other four were unharmed. Though their dirty cheeks were streaked with tears, they were smiling.

"Great plan, Nolan," Van said, lifting his bound hands over his head and thrusting down into his stomach. The locking mechanism snapped in two, and he rubbed the red marks on his wrists. "With added help from your alpha's tech," he said to me.

Nolan, Zed, and River broke free of their bindings but I didn't think I could get my hands over my head with as much as it was pounding. I let my head rest on the aluminum siding.

"Remington, think you can stop at the drug store? I think Wynn needs a painkiller," River asked, tapping the metal grating that separated us from the front seats.

Magnus turned around instead from his spot in the passenger seat. "He needs a hospital," he snarled. I knew his anger wasn't directed toward anyone in the van. Right about then, I was beginning to agree with his opinions of our plan. I was lucky he'd stayed quiet for as long as he had.

"I'll be f—"

"Don't say it," Magnus ordered darkly.

"Don't worry," Remington said, taking the exit that would bring them to the highway. "We'll get him checked out. We need to dump the van and get back to the OAC now anyway."

Later, the police would find their missing van intact, and I hoped they would have found the two officers Remington had to subdue to take their spots before that. Remington had left them bound but unharmed in a gas station bathroom, sans uniforms. After Magnus had made the anonymous call to the police regarding a possible omega kidnapping, the two had waited for the call for their transport unit to be brought to the scene. Thankfully, the officer in charge hadn't questioned how quickly the van was there.

"Do you think the founders will listen to us?" Van asked. "Once the cops realize we're missing, I don't think they'll be able to keep Taft for long."

"It won't matter if they listen to you" Magnus replied. "I modified the omega chip so that it tracked Wynn's location—allowing us to anonymously send the police in the right direction—and to record audio only. Wynn was recording the whole time. If they don't believe what's happened the first time they hear it, they can rewind the files and listen again."

Our eyes met, and while Magnus's face was still tight with anger, there was relief there as well. I smiled, the truth of what we'd just accomplished settling in slowly. I hadn't let myself think about the life possibly growing inside of me while there'd been work to do. If we hadn't taken down Taft, the baby wouldn't have lived long. But, right now, I knew that me and Magnus were thinking the same thing.

"Even if you all showed up at the station with full confessions, Taft wouldn't be detained for long," Remington said. "He couldn't set up the operation he did without a little outside help—alpha crime rings that want more power than they already have. And I imagine that outside help will discover what we've done sooner rather than later and send their lawyers. But, by then, the entire OAC will be aware. We'll protect our own, like always." Remington accelerated down the highway. I hoped he was driving away from the life I was leaving behind and toward a Tylenol.

CHAPTER SIXTEEN
Wynn

"You're glowing!" a stranger shouted at me in the packed bakery. Beside me, Magnus tensed and inched closer.

"I'm pregnant, yes," I said to the too-loud stranger standing so close to me I knew they'd had onions in their breakfast. Lots of onions. They also didn't understand the concept of personal space, either, as the man stepped to my other side and thrust his hand out as if to touch my rounded stomach.

I grabbed his wrist, keeping his hand from traveling the last few inches.

"Be nice," Magnus warned while sliding between us. "My omega doesn't like to be touched," he said kindly but firmly while prying my grip from the other man's arm.

The man stepped back, rubbing his wrist. He was lucky. The old me would've broken it. "You should teach your omega to not be so rude," he said with a pout.

I growled, but Magnus was still standing between us like a shield. "I do not agree. You should realize that your bodies are your own and you get a say in who touches you. You didn't ask. You assumed."

The line had moved in front of us, and it was our turn at the counter, but Magnus waved the handsy omega forward.

He gave the two of us angry, if not a little confused, looks, but trudged forward.

"If he takes the last of the salted caramel cupcakes, I'm blaming you," I hissed.

Magnus just blinked slowly and smiled. "You're so beautiful when you're angry."

I scowled. "I'm not angry, I'm hungry."

"You're beautiful when you're hungry too," he replied, reaching for his phone in the next second. He read the message, tapped out a reply, and sighed. "The merger is done. Lloyd reported the last of the paperwork has been signed."

A month-long deal was finally complete and now Magnus could begin the process of disassembling Visadore and selling the assets while retaining any employees he believed could be loyal to him. After the thing with Taft, Magnus had taken the proof he had from the memory stick of Visadore ordering a hit to their CEO. The slimy alpha acted shocked, but when Magnus started talking about the press, he became very agreeable. Magnus offered him a lower price than the CEO was likely expecting, but he accepted on the caveat that Magnus would forget about the tiny part where he tried to have him killed.

The way it had gone down still annoyed me, but it wasn't as if I could do anything in the shape I was in. Even when my bump had been tiny, the added weight had thrown off my balance. I wasn't helpless, but I wasn't exactly operating in stealth mode these days either.

Not to mention the fact that I had to pee nearly constantly. And the hormones had taken some getting used to. After the night Magnus came back to the penthouse, riddled with holes in the walls from where I'd spent the afternoon and evening hunting a fly that would not stop buzzing in my ear, he'd started working from home. And hid most of the kitchen knives.

The omega in front of us turned back around, his arms weighed down with bags of pastries and treats. "I'm sorry," he said to me as he passed. "You were right. But you're still glowing," he added like he'd called me a name.

I was too shocked to reply, but Magnus's face spoke volumes. He smiled so wide it looked like he was trying to touch his ears. "See, the world can learn. We can teach it. With words."

We stepped up to the counter, and Magnus ordered three dozen donuts and coffee enough for an army. "And two salted caramel cupcakes, please," he added at the end.

"You want one?" I asked Magnus as the attendant rushed around the cases, fulfilling his order.

"No, I just know you. You'll finish the first and immediately ask for another."

"You're trying to fatten me up. I'm already your mate. You don't have to trap me."

The attendant placed the first of our boxes on the counter.

Magnus stood behind me, reaching his hands around my front and resting them on my belly. "I pity the fool who tries," he murmured, kissing my ear after.

That time, it was my phone that drew my attention. "It's Remington. I'll wait outside?"

A dark cloud settled over his head, but he eventually nodded. "Sure."

"Have you heard anything?" I said instead of hello.

We'd been correct in assuming Taft wouldn't have been held for long. In fact, it ended up being less than three hours that he'd remained in a cell while his lawyers threw their weight around. At least now we knew a little more about where Taft had come from now that we knew who had stepped up to defend him. By the time he'd made it to the OAC campus, Remington had the place on lockdown. No one got in or out until the founders had a chance to review our information.

They'd interviewed us all, including Magnus, and returned with the message that they were appointing Remington as temporary director of the OAC and that

192

Taft would be dealt with. Considering how we never heard from him after that day, I didn't need long to guess how he'd been dealt with. It seemed for a bit that everything was going according to plan, until I submitted my request for resignation from the OAC.

"The internal audit has been completed," Remington replied. "As we hoped, you were the first omega sent on an unsanctioned hit. No other alphas lost their lives unnecessarily." He needed the caveat because the OAC still operated as it had, eliminating alphas when it was necessary. And I still believed in that cause, but now, I was ready to help in a different way.

"That's a relief. And the other request?" I spotted Magnus through the shop windows, paying for the sweets before lifting the boxes and heading toward me. His backup plans had backup plans when it came to what we would do if the OAC rejected my resignation. I just wished we wouldn't have to use any of them.

"The founders weren't willing to make more personnel changes at this time," Remington said quickly. "So I reminded them that their incompetence and inability to spot a rat had placed not just you but the entire OAC in danger."

"And?"

"And you're a former assassin."

While it was what I'd wanted, the moment still felt bittersweet.

"They would like to keep you on as a consultant. There are going to be a lot of changes happening, and we agree on this that your opinion in the matter would be priceless. They have put a price on it, though. I'll send the position details so you and your alpha can discuss it."

I thanked Remington, setting up a time for us to talk further. When Magnus joined me on the sidewalk, I reached out to help relieve him of his load, but he shook his head. "You're always carrying something for me," he said before studying my face. "They said no," he growled.

"Not really, but sort of. I'm out of the field. No more missions."

The dark cloud cleared. "You're too good at your job for them to let you go completely. I understand. I'll agree with whatever you decide, but right now, we have to head to class. Your students are waiting."

***

I stood at the head of the class, a wall of mirrors at my back and a row of students at my front.

"We aren't stronger than alphas," I announced to the class. About twenty in total stood shoulder to shoulder in loose workout gear. In the back, Magnus was there munching on a donut with the other alphas who had come to watch their omegas train. "And while I can't do anything to change that, I can give us a different sort of power."

A hand rose from an omega with violently red hair. "But you're pregnant," he said softly.

"I am, and I'll have to make adjustments, but my point still stands—"

"But what can you do if you're pregnant?" the omega asked, not bothering to raise his hand.

My eyes landed on the face of an alpha in the back who looked like he was battling pride with embarrassment.

"Is that your alpha?" I asked the redheaded omega. He turned toward the direction I pointed and nodded.

"That's Tom. He's probably thinking this is one of those times I should stay quiet," he said with a sad smile.

I moved close enough to clap my hand on his shoulder. "Don't talk down on yourself for asking questions. It's important. And, I'd even guess its a reason why Tom liked you in the first place."

Tom nodded, even though his cheeks burned red.

"Tom's a big alpha," I said to the omega who smiled.

"He's so strong," he said with stars in his eyes.

"Do you mind if I use him?"

The omega's eyes bulged. "Like, to attack you? No, no,

he'll hurt you just on accident."

"Let's see." I backed up so that I stood in the middle of the exercise room. The mats were brand new and still stiff. I motioned for Tom to come forward, which caused a wave of hooting and whistling from the rest of the alphas. They were good men—they wouldn't have brought their omegas to an omega defense class if they weren't—but that didn't mean they believed that an omega could actually defend himself. And all they knew of me was that I was Magnus's mate.

When Tom breached the crowd and stepped into the clear space, I crouched down. "Attack me," I told him.

"Are you sure?" Tom asked, looking to Magnus, who nodded unhappily.

Tom gave me a doubtful look before tucking his head down and charging toward me like a football player. I stepped to the side, and he sailed past me. "Try again," I called out to his back. "But for reals this time." That turned some of the hoots into laughs, and Tom squared up with me once more, determination in his stance that wasn't there before.

He charged forward, intending to grab me around the middle. I settled on the balls of my feet, listening to my breath whoosh out as I felt the weight of my belly at my front. When he was almost on top of me, I turned to the side and ducked, Tom landed against my back, and I grabbed his arm. Keeping his weight where I needed it to be able to stand, I used his forward momentum to roll him off my back, over my shoulders, and down on the ground. I kept a hold of his arm when he landed, jamming my foot into his armpit and twisting.

"From here, I can break his arm and run or hold him here if help is near."

For a moment, there was only silence. In the back, Magnus began to applaud, setting off a wave of cheering from alpha, omega, and beta alike.

The redheaded omega rushed forward, helping me pull

Tom to his feet. He shook my hand while wrapping the other arm over his omega's shoulders. "Do you have package deals?" Tom asked.

There were no more questions debating my ability to lead the class, which was good because it still took two hours to cover the basics. We worked on how to stand when out in public and how to remain aware of what was going on around you. By the end of the class, the donuts and coffee were gone, I was exhausted, and everyone had signed up for next week's class. Some had gone ahead and paid for the whole set.

Magnus took the bag of trash out of my hands and lifted me, setting me down gently on a pile of mats in the corner. "You did amazing work today, babe," Magnus said, reaching for my foot. He began to massage, and the moan that escaped my lips was entirely indecent.

"You're the one who gave me this space, did the marketing. That was nice of your friends to help canvass the neighborhoods."

"Well, they'd already seen what you could do. They believe in creating a more equal world. They also said they were sorry to miss this class but are bringing their omegas to the next one." He kept rubbing, and we sat there in silence. "Are you happy, Wynn? Today brought big changes."

I hadn't known at the time, but my days with the OAC had all prepared me for this. Before, I'd been too angry. I wouldn't have been able to be what Magnus needed in a mate. But the OAC and his patience had helped form me. "I'm where I should be, Magnus. With the alpha I should be with."

He smiled and kept massaging, switching to the other foot so that I wouldn't "walk crooked."

I settled into the mat, my hands on my belly, when I felt the strangest feeling. A fluttering movement, like gas, but inherently more meaningful. I gasped.

"What? What is it? You pushed yourself too hard?"

"No, worrywart, feel."

I grabbed his hand and pressed it over the flutter. He waited patiently as a full minute passed before it happened again. "Is that?" he gasped, and I smiled.

We sat that way for several long moments, a family experiencing a first. There would be more to come. Labor was over a month away. Then there would be first bottles, first diapers, first words, first steps. So many things to look forward to. Before, if anyone had asked me if I planned on settling down, on finding a family, I would've laughed. Why would I have wanted to bring life into the world I knew?

But now that I knew what it was like to be loved by a good man, to have a pack family that stood by you even when your path took you from them. Why would I want to bring new life in this world rife with fear and hate?

Because I was omega enough to protect what was mine.

ACKNOWLEDGMENTS

Fervor came at the worst time. But sometimes, a book refuses to be ignored. Wynn and Magnus demanded to have their story told but it would not have been possible without the help and guidance of my editor, M.A. Hinkle of Les Court Services. Your keen eye is always much appreciated. An equally huge, amazing, you are so wonderful, thank you to my beta readers, Jena you are now a permanent part of my process and Kirk with Les Court services—your enthusiasm and comments helped get me through the rough parts! As always, a huge thank you to my cover artist, Adrien Rose (https://bit.ly/2AbXVcx). You amaze me! Thank you to my family, for understanding that when I say I'm listening, I'm lying unless I am looking at them. To my writing family for keeping me ambitious and motivated and always, to the readers for being the reason why I write!

ABOUT THE AUTHOR

Kiki Burrelli lives in the Pacific Northwest with the bears and raccoons. She dreams of owning a pack of goats that she can cuddle and dress in form-fitting sweaters. Kiki loves writing and reading and is always chasing that next character that will make her insides shiver. Consider getting to know Kiki at her website, kikiburrelli.net, on Facebook, in her Facebook fan group or send her an email to kiki@kikiburrelli.net

FERVOR